THE

DOWN LOW
DIARIES

**ALSO BY
ERIC WARE:**

THE HOLLYWOOD COLORED

THE

DOWN LOW DIARIES

ERIC WARE

WAREWORD PUBLISHING

Published by Wareword Publishing
www.warewordpublishing.com

Library of Congress Catalogue Card Number: 2006938858
Ware, Eric
The Down Low Diaries / Eric Ware

ISBN 978-0-9740704-1-4

SAN: 255-3635

Printed in the United States of America
First Printing

This is dedicated to everybody
who felt the need to hide.

Early Withdrawal

I don't want a damn thing to do with you. I mean, what *don't* you understand about that?

"But why?" she said. "I just don't get it."

"That's ok," I said. "I get it enough for the both of us." She didn't say anything and looked dramatically off into space. Too bad for her I wasn't in the mood for drama. I hate drama. Despise it. From now on it's nothing but comedy for the kid. Action and adventure. Maybe romance. A big maybe. But no drama. And now I was bored. Bored of her staring at the rushing traffic, bored with caucasians eying us like potential robbers as we stood there blocking the door to the bank, and bored with the gray clouds that coasted against the whitewashed sky. Rain already. "Well, if you ain't gonna say nothing, I gotta go."

"Wait. How could you do this to me?"

"Do what to you? You're a grown-ass woman," I said almost whining. She was winning the drama war despite my best efforts to be immune. Immune. What a funny word. Nothing

1

can get to you. Nothing can hurt you. Nothing can affect you for the worst. Immune. What a funny little made-up word.

She started to cry, of course. Bravely holding her head back to blink back the tears and all that. But it was just more drama for my benefit. People who really don't want to cry, simply don't. Damn, I hate this bitch. And I hate myself for the pain I cause her. And that makes me hate her even more.

"I told you from the jump that I was into men, too. You said, fine. You was a modern 'round the way kind of gal. You remember that, Kim? Look at me goddamnit. You remember?" She sucked her bottom lip like a stupid child and nodded her head. "You said you was fine with it. Freaked a few times yourself back in college. In the drama department." That should have warned me right there. "You said as long as I didn't give you a disease, and wore a rubber, you were cool with it." I hate it when women say that. Like I'm running around like Lex Luthor trying to figure out the best way to give them AIDS. They seem to forget there's still a chance I could catch it from them, too. And yeah, I've heard the stories about these DL sissies giving women HIV, but that's not me, and I'm tired of hearing about it. I don't remember *Essence* magazine devoting two back-to-back issues to AIDS when faggots were the ones dying from it. Besides, women don't mind keeping it on the down low when *they're* the ones sleeping with another woman's man, now do they?

And now it started to rain. Pathetic.

I wasn't about to stand out there and argue in the rain the way people do in the movies so I grabbed her by the arm and pulled her into the lobby of the bank. It was a wide, marbled space with the security guard's booth in the center of the floor and different little overpriced shops lined the sides. The bank was up on the third floor.

We sat down on a metal bench with minimal cushioning to avoid the rush of damp people running in from the storm outside. I caught our images in the mirror on the opposite wall and we looked like we were together. Like a couple, I mean. That's what people used to tell us when they saw us at a club, a party, or even the mall. "Yall, look like an old married couple." It was fun to enjoy the fantasy. I'd be lying if I said I hadn't wished for a normal life with a wife, kids, and PTA meetings. "Yall look like an old married couple," they'd say. And I suppose we did. To strangers. Now the mirror was saying the same thing. Mirrors lie.

I sat there watching her reflection snivel into balled-up pieces of tissue. Doesn't anybody in the free world, besides me, carry a handkerchief anymore? My mother always told me to carry a handkerchief and I always did. I suppose I should have offered Kim my handkerchief, like a gentleman, but it was perfect, clean and white. I didn't want her snot and mascara messing all that up.

That's when he walked by. That security guard that I've been scoping for the past month or so. I see him every time I come in here to cash my check. Fine-ass nigga, too. I got hard just looking at him. He saw me checking him out and gave me that tough thug nod that they do. It's a nod that's halfway saying "hey" but not quite committed enough to be friendly. That's all right though, player. You know what time it is. I'm not one of these men with infallible gay-dar. I *have* made mistakes. Sometimes straight boys make eye contact, too. Learned that the hard way. And sometimes these Bi-boys know good and well they're checking you out but, if you make a move, they start acting all offended and hard. Please. You're not mad at me, you're mad at the faggot in yourself. But this security guard was giving all the right signals and I'd been letting him marinate for a while. Damn. Look at those juicy football player haunches. Yeah. You getting laid today, Mr. Security. I've been through a lot and I deserve some ass today. But first, I gotta ditch the dead weight.

I looked in the mirror and saw Kim looking at me. Then she looked at Mr. Security and back at me.

"That's your bus, right?" I said. She looked back at Mr. Security and, sure enough, the bus schedules were posted on his booth. I been doing this a while, baby.

"Oh, uh, yeah," she said. "But I rode my bike today."

"Well you can't ride it back in this rain."

"It'll let up. It always does."

"Uh-huh." I hope the guard doesn't go on break before she stops talking.

"I just don't understand why we can't keep things going like they were before." *'Cause I like dick more than you do, that's why.* "I don't care about your... activities... I have my other men, too." *That's a lie. If you had other men you wouldn't be acting so goddamn desperate.*

"It's me, Kim. I just need space." Mr. Security was giving this Paris Hilton knock-off directions and checked her out while she walked away. I didn't know if that was for my benefit or not. He looked at me then went back to reading his paper. "And I'm sorry I've been so short." He dropped the paper he was reading. Please bend over. "None of this is fair to you." Please, God, make him bend over. In Jesus' Name I pray. Amen. "But

I need some time to sort things out." He bent over. Whoever makes those skintight security uniforms needs a special award from the fashion industry. "It's probably best we spend some time apart."

"So…" She stuffed her tissues in her jeans and kept her eyes on the floor. "So what you're saying is… you just need time?" He straightened back up and I didn't even pretend I wasn't looking. "This isn't a break-up? Just a break?" Which answer would make her go away?

"Yeah. That's what I'm saying." She let out a laugh that sounded like a quivering sigh and hugged me on the bench. He looked at us both and turned away. *Get your damn hands off me.* "All right, Kim. All right. Easy now."

"Excuse me, mister man, I forgot how you are about public displays of affection." I laughed a fake laugh and wished I had magic powers like Endora so I could pop this bitch into the next county. "So I will be on my way and call you, um, let's see, next week too soon?"

"I'll call you," I said. A flash of worry crossed her face and for a second I felt like shit but just for a second. "I'll call you. I promise." The words, I promise, are like a lullaby to the brains of desperate women that rocks their reason to sleep. They seem to think they've got you if you say, I promise, and will generally go away after that.

"Ok. Well, bye then. Oh, look," she said and pointed outside. "It stopped raining." And so it had. The pigeons felt bold enough to attack soggy chunks of bread on the sidewalk and slow drips of water fell from the awnings. "Told you it would let up." Poor thing saw it as some sort of sign. Oh well. She kissed me quick on the cheek and walked out the door. I watched her cross the street without permission from the traffic signal and unlock her bike. She waved at me through the tinted windows even though she couldn't see me. I didn't wave back. She got on her wet bike and headed down Fifth.

Finally. Out with the drama and in with the porn.

I took off my wind breaker so my tattoos would show through the Lakers throw-back jersey I had on. The lobby was crowded but I've always found it easier to hide in plain sight. I walked to the security booth eyeing my target all the way. Some skinny queen by the elevator was trying to catch my eye. I think I recognized him from the club but to hell with him. Too fem for me. If I wanted a woman I'd sleep with one.

Mr. Security saw me approaching and put down his paper.

"What's up?" he said

"What's up with you?"

"Can I help you?" Oh, so he wants to play hard to get.

"What time you get off?"

"Say what now?"

"I said: What. Time. You. Get. Off. You hear me better now?"

He looked suspicious and angry. "Why you want to know, man?"

" 'Cause I want to be there when it happens."

"When what happens?"

"When you get off." He stared at me. He glanced around to see who was looking. Then he eyed my crotch. Yeah. I knew you was ripe.

He was jet black with muscles that stretched his uniform. He sported a neat mustache surrounding thick lips and star-white teeth. He kind of looked like Richard T. Jones and I'd lick *that* nigga 'til he shined. "What's your name?" he said.

"Man, it don't even matter." He smiled in a way that told me he understood and put a sign up on the counter that said, *Back in ten minutes.* "Give me a little credit, player."

"It's all the time I got," he said with a laugh. "Come on." I followed him to the stairwell by the elevator. "Right this way," he said. He sounded very official all of the sudden for the bene-fit of passersby. It wasn't necessary. If it's one thing I've learned in this down low life it's that straight people never paid atten-tion to anything.

We entered the stairwell and I watched his behind bounce from side to side as we climbed the stories. "Where you work out at?" I said.

"Gold's. You?"

"Bally's." I grabbed his belt to slow him down and palmed him with my other hand. He let out a breath, like he touched something hot, and I stepped up the stairs and pressed myself against him. I tilted his head back and sucked the side of his salty neck. He reached back and rubbed me through my pants.

"Not yet," he said. He pulled away from my insistent grip and kept on up two more flights. I was way too hard for all this walking. Just when I started to complain we stopped at a sign that said, *Third Floor.* If I kept right through that door I would be in the hallway that led to the bank. Next to that, was another door with chains and a combination lock on it. Mr. Security fiddled with the lock while I wondered what was going on. I just figured we were going to a restroom like I do at the airport, or the park, or just freak in the stairwell like I've done at the mall.

The lock clicked open, the chain slid off the steel handle, and he pushed open the door to a dark, hot room. Right away the smell of sex hit my nostrils. He grabbed my wrist and pulled me inside. A warm wave crossed my stomach like I was on a roller coaster. He closed the door without turning on the light and shoved me against the wall. He pinched my nipples with rude aggression and crammed his tongue in my mouth.

There's nothing like kissing a man. Nothing. Straight fellas always say, "How can somebody be a sissy with all these bitches around?" Bitch, please. How can you be straight with all these men around? Fuck you. I'm sleeping with Kim right now out of habit and expectation more than anything else. I'm far from coming out of the closet because of my job and other reasons. And even though Kim can still make me come, I'm quickly sliding down the slope from Bi to Homo. It's just a matter of time.

A woman can't kiss me like this. It's impossible. Another pair of wet lips, just as thick as mine, mashing into my face, brushing against my mustache, sucking my tongue with the same force that I suck his. What can I say?

I appreciated the way he was pinching my nipples. Nipples are one of those things on your body that nobody can touch the way you can. Not perfectly. But Mr. Security was the next best thing to being me. And as for a woman? Forget about it. Women never touch your nipples unless you ask them to and who wants to do that? On the rare occasion that a girl does touch your nipples just right, you don't want to act too pleased about it, because who wants to look like a fag?

Anyway.

I guided his hands below my waist where they belonged. Meanwhile, I cupped that round butt of his and squeezed. He moaned so I slapped it and got the same reaction, even louder. I heard the elevator ding outside. The echoed voices of three or four people laughed as they headed towards the bank. I hesitated.

"Don't worry 'bout it, baby," he said. "I do this all the time." He kissed me again and that eased my nerves. He knew what I wanted and loosened his belt. I reached down through the slack of his pants and felt his hot naked skin. No underwear. I nuzzled my stubble against his cheek and stuck my tongue in his ear. "Oh yeah, daddy." Daddy? I've been doing Kim all week and was kinda looking forward to somebody boning me for a change. But if he wants me to be the daddy then that's cool.

"Suck my dick." I was surprised how loud my voice was. He dropped like gravity and pulled me free of my Hanes.

"Damn, daddy," he said just a little surprised.

"Yeah, that's all yours, baby." He licked the hole and made me jump. His mouth was so hot and hungry. He bobbed back and forth, and with each new motion, he got sweeter and closer to the base. He knew how to use his tongue underneath so it would work in unison with his lips. He knew how to actually inhale and not just go back and forth without purpose. He knew how to keep his teeth out the way so that all I felt was wet softness. And he knew how to keep on rubbing my nipples without me telling him to.

It was a blow job only an angel could give.

I grabbed him by the back of his head and rammed his mouth like an inmate. He never ran away from it. I heard him squeal and then he squirted on my thigh. When I felt him reach his climax I lost it in his mouth. He was squeezing one of his nipples and I should have been nice and squeezed the other one for him but when I'm coming I can only think of myself.

His walkie-talkie squawked and scared us. There was an older man's voice on the other end. "Anderson. Where you at?" He put his finger to his lips in warning and I nodded that I'd remain silent.

"What?" said Anderson. He had an attitude and I gathered he didn't like the other guy.

"Where you at?" The voice said.

"Third Floor." *Why tell him the truth, you moron?* You could have been anywhere in this entire building. What if he came looking for you or was on the third floor himself? Stupid answer, Anderson. Just plain dumb.

"I'll be there in a second. You at the bank?"

"Uh, yeah."

"Okay. Here I come." Anderson hopped to his feet in a panic and pulled up his pants.

"We gotta go."

"No shit."

"Damn. That's a damn shame." He was starring at my privates in fascination and zipped up his pants. I was still hard. "Hurry up, man." I tucked myself into my pants as best I could. He cracked the door to make sure the coast was clear and I looked at the stained mattress. Who else would be lying there tomorrow or even later today? Not that I was jealous or anything. I just wondered. "Come on," he said. I stepped outside and he locked the door. The elevator opened and the older security guard stepped into the hall. He saw us standing close together so I looked at Anderson and said,

"Where's the bank? I've been going up and down that elevator forever."

"Right through those double doors," said Anderson. He even managed a professional smile.

"Thank you." I left him there and wished we had more time to exchange numbers, or e-mails, or something else beside bodily fluids. But, hey. I knew where he worked. The double doors closed behind me while the older guard talked about something that I'm sure was very important. I went inside the bank to cash my check. There was a very long line but I really didn't mind.

2

Salsa in my Chocolate

I despise this city. But everything original about hating LA has already been said so let's skip all that. I had to come here for my job and I like having money. I'm not rich or anything but all of my needs and most of my wants are met. I suppose that's something to be grateful for. All the self-help books say that if you don't notice the little things then the Universe won't give you the big things. Whatever. I just needs to get laid.

Up the ass this time.

And since I'm in LA, I'd like some salsa in my chocolate. I'm a proud black man. I adore my brothers and lay them frequently but there's something about those delicious Latino gangsters that just makes me happy and gay.

I know you've seen that Venezuelan dude on *That 70s Show*. Have you ever seen him when he ain't playing that goofy-ass part? Now that's some fine Latino beefcake and the reason you can call him a wetback is because I'm licking his ass. In my dreams, that is. I'll be reincarnated as his skin-tight pants if I live my life right. Yeah. That's a fine motherfucker right there. No doubt. And Lindsay Lohan had some of that? That's a lucky bitch. They're not dating any more and I don't know how she messed that up. She really must be crazy, after all. Hell. I'd let that man fuck me into a diabetic coma 'cause that's a sticky sweet stud right there.

Ricky Ricardo was a fine bastard, too. What the hell was Lucy always bitching about? Do you think I'd give a damn about being in the show if I was married to Ricky Ricardo? That fine motherfucker *is* the show and his dick is the main attraction. And Melanie Griffith? That loopy-ass heifer was sleeping with Antonio Banderas and she wound up in rehab. Bitch, why the hell ain't you happy? You are receiving pipe from Zorro himself. What seems to be the goddamn problem? If you want to get high so bad then stick his dick up your ass and make the mark of the "Z." If *that* won't alter your mood then nothing will. These crazy white bitches don't know what to do with these Latino men.

But I do.

And I knew just where I could find one. There's this Puerto Rican that I've been playing eye tag with for weeks. The Bally gym on Gower has a bit of a reputation but I've been staying out of the steam room lately where all the action takes place. I used to go swimming there and scope out men in the pool but, let's face it, even though a lot of homos go to Bally's it's not a gay gym, per se, like something in West Hollywood or even on Hyperion. After the media exploitation of down low hysteria, it's made it harder for the rest of us to maintain our cover. Did you see Oprah Winfrey treating that fool like he discovered the cure for AIDS when all this down low mess first started? I could tell he was gay as soon as he opened his mouth but his own wife couldn't? Ok then. The point is you have to be careful scoping in Bally's if you're on the DL.

The best thing to do is to use the mirrors for more than just reflection. You don't make eye contact with the man. Instead, you make eye contact with the mirror. The mirror is your friend. You can check out somebody at your leisure without looking like you're looking. Now, if a man spots you looking at him in the mirror then you've got several options. If he's straight... that's cool. He'll either look away, because he doesn't want you to think he's a fag, or he'll assume you're admiring his muscles. Many people don't believe it, and I wish it weren't true, but there are plenty of straight bodybuilders. They're used to being stared at, and even welcome it, so they don't get all freaked out when another man eyes them. Now, if for some reason the straight muscle boy gets all offended and gives you that glare, all you have to do is say something like, "I been trying to get my lats to flare out like that for months. You make me sick." The straight guy will undoubtedly laugh and give you tips about your lats now that his ego has been stroked. Bodybuilders love to talk about building bodies. However, keep the conversation short. You're looking for a butt buddy. Not a workout buddy.

The preferred second option is that the man who spots your reflected desire likes sleeping with other men, too. That's perfect but not complete. Because another gay man, especially one on the low, will play more mind games with you than a chess pro. Especially if he wants you. That's what I've been going through with the latest object of my desire: Dante.

Dante knows I want him and his dismissals are pissing me off. Every time I move in his direction he finds a reason to move away. He looks like he won the Mr. Hung Puerto Rican Contest five years in a row. I can tell by the way it swings because he never wears any drawers. He's Rick Fox brown with curly hair. He's got deep, crystal-ball eyes and he usually wears a wife beater that partially reveals a tattoo of Jesus on his chest. He always works out in these gray gym shorts that coaches wear. His butt is high and round, which make those shorts hug him properly when he's doing squats. This man is so fine he could sell his sweat. He's either married, or has a girlfriend, because he makes a big production of talking loud with some gal on the cell phone.

He never makes eye contact with me. Not even if I sit on the leg press machine right next to him. In fact, Dante's one of those boys that try just a bit too hard not to look. I can understand him pulling that pose on the sissies. Who wants to give a punk the wrong idea or the slightest encouragement? They'll take that and run with it. Wanna know how to propose to a sissy? You say hello. But, I don't really appreciate Dante pulling that stunt with me.

I ain't no fucking faggot.

Today, I was determined to get him, though. I had given myself an enema so there wouldn't be any embarrassing moments. I hate getting shit on my dick. Hate it. If you know you like to get fucked up the ass, then for God's Sake, please take some basic precautions. That's just common sense. Straight folks might call us shit packers but I assure you I don't like looking at my own feces much less anybody else's. My asshole is Pine Sol clean and I expect the same from others. Okay. Enough of my preaching.

I spotted Dante running on the treadmill next to that little fat guy he works out with who was just walking on the treadmill next to him. I didn't know if that guy was his cousin or what.

Maybe Dante did personal training on the side. I've seen him give the fat boy specific training tips and he seems deeply concerned about Chuckles' progress. Chuckles was a Latino too but I ain't busting open no piñatas. Damn it. This was all I needed. A big, fat cock blocker in the way. Dante's already skittish so I dare not approach him in front of somebody. The good news, however, is that Dante might be a personal trainer and that's the gayest profession since interior design.

I approached them from behind. They were on the squat rack and Chuckles was gasping for breath doing reps with a ninety pound load. Dante encouraged him on:

"C'mon, papi, six more. I got you." I loved his voice. It rumbled like a gentle scold. "Five more, papi. Keep it pumping, keep it pumping." He put a steadying hand on Chuckle's back who strained and breathed heavier by the second. Please don't let this fat boy pass out or something. That'd be a great way to set the mood.

"How many more sets yall got?" I said. Dante looked at me with the nonchalance of slight contempt and said,

"Two." Then, he turned back to Chuckles. Looks like I'm going to have to work for this one. The fat boy was breathing like he had to remember how.

"How many reps you say I have left again?" Chuckles said.

"Don't know," said Dante. He gave me a look. "I lost count." Oh, ok. So that's how it is.

I moved by the leg press machine next to them and stretched while making sure my backside faced the mirror. I got a nice ass. It's not a ghetto booty or anything but it sticks out in a plump curve going up and away from my back and it looks great without clothes. There are hardly any lines on my bottom thanks to fanatic applications of Ambi. My anus is tighter than a miser's fist. Guys love that. Especially guys with kids. Even the woman who keeps in great shape is going to lose some elasticity after a few kids. There's no way you can pass something the size of a bowling ball through your vagina two or three times and be the same tight fit you were back in college. No way in hell.

I don't want to reduce the complexity of being gay to the size of an asshole but many married women don't want anal sex. They think it's repellent and they give themselves a big pat on the back for bothering to give their husbands a blow job in the first place. That's enough, they figure, and they've done their marital duty now who wants eggs? If these prudish hens would simply give themselves an enema, the same way they douche out their bloody birth canal, and take their husband's wiener between the buns like a good girl, then they might see a noticeable reduction in straying. At least, that's what these married suckers always tell me. "Damn. Your ass so tight. Hell, yeah. This better than pussy here. Aw fuck, yeah. If my wife did this I wouldn't be here, motherfucker. Now, take this big dick. Take it, faggot!" That reminds me. I need to give Tyrone a call. On the other hand, if Tyrone, or any other man, just wanted anal sex, then I'm sure they could find or pay a woman to do that for them. No, these married men just don't want their dick in some ass. They want their dick in a man's ass.

A man like me.

So I bent over and grabbed my ankles for Dante's benefit. Nothing happened, not even a glance. That's a hostile bastard. I wonder if he's like that in bed? God, I hope so. I didn't want to be too obvious, and if I had any sense I'd be ashamed, but the only logical thing left to do was to simply take off my pants. I was wearing those track warm-up pants that you get out of Target that snap apart in one whisk. So I just whisked those babies off myself and there I stood in the full glory of my He-bitch pants. The He-bitch pants are tight, tight shorts, riding Daisy Duke high, made of a cotton-spandex blend, through a wonderful technology that I don't care about and you don't either. God just bless the nerd who invented them, that's all.

My He-bitch pants are a powder blue second skin. They're both a calling card and a warning. A defiant invitation to the crack of my ass. They're the devil's advertisement of the ebony goodies bulging from within. I don't normally wear my He-bitch pants unless I'm going to the steam room or maybe at home to tease a thug coming over for the first time. They almost scream "faggot" and the only straight men who wear them are probably Olympic athletes and circus folk.

I never wear them in the gym, unless I'm visiting Santa Monica Boulevard, because I might see a woman I know in here or some guys from the bowling alley. But to hell with it. I called in sick and every straight person I know is at work this time of day. In fact, in the early afternoon, the only people in Bally's are the unemployed actors, kept women, and the unemployed models. So I thought I could take the risk. I had to. I needed some bad.

It felt so warm inside there when I was fingering myself in the shower this morning. That's what Tyrone is always saying, too. In addition to marveling about how tight I am, compared to his wife, he always says, "Damn, bitch. Your pussy so fucking hot. Aw, fuck yeah. How you keep this pussy so hot for daddy, hmm?" Now, Tyrone knows good and well that I don't like him calling my asshole a pussy. I guess it's the big, dumb nigga's way of holding on to the vestiges of being straight. If he can talk that way loud enough when he's sleeping with me then it's not really like he's lying with a man. That's why some fellas are strictly into drag queens. Sometime, Tyrone talks to me in bed the way I talk to Kim. I don't know. I guess I kind of understand it.

He doesn't want to think about what he's doing. Degrading me helps justify his behavior and pardons his lust. But I kicked that fool out of my house the last time and told him, "If you want some pussy so bad then go home to your wore-out wife!" Still. If he's stroking me just right, and hitting that spot... and if I'm high enough and about to come anyway... I'll let him get away with it.

I stood wide and bent over giving my hamstrings a stretch. I looked between my legs and caught Chuckles staring at my ass like he hadn't eaten in days. Wrong menu, Shamu. I straightened back up, and turned around, and Dante was looking at me like he could kill me. He had me worried but then he gave me the nod. He'd never nodded at me before.

"Yall done?" I asked.

"One more set," Dante said a little nicer than before.

"I'm done, man," Chuckles said.

"Quit being a bitch, yo." They argued a little in Spanish and I recalled that *Spanish Made Easy* CD in my car that I never listened to. Dante said something very forcefully to Chuckles and, for some reason, the fat boy walked off in a huff. Finally. Now I could ask him for—

"You need a spot, homes?" He beat me to it. I was shocked and I guess it showed because then he looked liked he regretted asking. He scanned the gym to see who was there. I knew that look and did a quick check myself. We were mostly by ourselves in the free-weight section and almost everybody else was upstairs. It wouldn't stay that way forever, of course, and somebody could see from the track above if they were looking that hard but— "Yo, you deaf or something, man? You want a spot or not?"

"Yeah. Thanks."

"How much weight you want on here?"

"Add another forty-five. Thanks." We each added a forty-five pound plate to our respective sides of the bar in silence.

"You want this?" he said. He held up the foam neck protector.

"No, I like feeling the bar on my back." I laughed and he stared at me. I didn't feel the same sense of control I felt back at the bank. I was aggressive and confident with Mr. Security but with Dante I was... insecure. I stepped into my place under the bar. I placed both hands on the steel and didn't move.

"You need help already?" he said. The impatience was back in his voice.

"Just a little," I lied. What was I going to do next? Drop my handkerchief? He stepped closer behind me and grabbed the bar.

"Ready?"

"Yeah." I backed up against him and he stepped away. So I began my squat.

"One," he said. "Keep your head up." I nodded and blew my breath out with force. I came back up and clenched my butt cheeks hard. Not just to entice him but because that's the way you're supposed to do squats. Really. "Two," he said. I went back down and looked around in the mirror. I saw Chuckles up above us, on the second floor, walking around the track while everybody ran past him. He looked so alone. I almost felt sorry for him. "Three. That's right. Good form." We were still pretty much alone in the free weight area. "Four." The two senior citizens down here with us were making their way to the machines upstairs. The other fella with the headband on, who looked like he was here because he had a free pass, was moving on as well. "Five." Dante stared at my ass. "Six." Now all I had to do was figure out when was I going to need his help.

"I need help," I said with just a little worry in my voice. He stepped closer and put his hands on my waist.

"You need to stop, homes. I think you done."

"Uh-uh, man. I can do twenty of these."

"Ok, homes, I got you. Here we go." He stepped right up against me. "Seven." I squatted all the way down and paused there like I was having trouble.

"You done?" Dante said.

"No," I said. "I can do this. I know I can!" All very gung-ho. Very Rocky.

"Then move, nigga." He laughed a little. "You looks like you trying to lay a egg."

"Well spot me, damn it!" He reached his arms around me for support and I poked out to meet his groin. No doubt about it. He was hard all right. Our eyes met in the mirror and he gave me that mean look of his. We began our slow ascent together with him glued to my cotton-spandex homewreckers. With a cautionary browse, he was assured of our privacy as we came to standing. I clenched him between my ambidextrous globes and hit massage. He yanked me closer by my shorts, all the while, keeping lookout.

"Back up on that, bitch." He's a talker. I stood there and ground against something that felt like a forearm. "You like that, yeah?"

"Yeah."

"You want this, huh?"

"Oh, yeah."

"How much you want it, bitch?"

Then, I looked up into the mirror and saw Chuckles leaning against the rail staring down at us. "Psst. Dante!" He signaled us with a frantic wave. "Dante! Yall better cut that shit out. People coming, man." Dante felt me up all over and looked at Chuckles. He backed away, with a curse, while I adjusted my erection to a comfortable position. He stared at my glutes with regret and I put my track pants back on. Just then, a group of joggers passed by Chuckles on the track.

"Too bad," he said.

"Meet me in the showers."

"I don't mess around in the showers, homes."

"It's easy. We won't get caught. Come to the stall in the back on the left. If there's somebody else in there—" People filtered into the weight room and I lowered my voice. "—just chill out in the steam room if there's somebody in there. Then check the stall again in a few minutes or so."

"I don't do the steam room, homes. Too many faggots in the steam room."

"Look. You want it or not?" He didn't respond. More people entered so he picked up some dumbbells and exercised. I stretched in the mirror so it wouldn't just look like we were just standing there talking. I don't know why that would bother us. We could have easily been two straight men standing there talking. Women were coming in now and that made me uncomfortable. "I've got a yellow towel with a picture of Sponge Bob on it," I whispered to Dante. "I'll drape that over the stall so you'll know it's me." He continued his bicep curls without acknowledgment of my existence. There were people around now and things were back to normal.

I left without looking at him and hoped he would follow. I didn't normally do the showers myself but I was willing to make an exception for him. I went to the water fountain and passed Chuckles coming down on the stairs. He nodded at me and for some reason I didn't nod back. There was a line at the fountain because some jerk was filling up his enormous water jug. I watched Chuckles say something to Dante and they both stared at me. I looked away. The considerate fella with the jug moved on and the line inched up a bit. I saw Dante reach into his bag and pull out a fresh T-shirt. He took off his wife beater and this woman elbowed her girlfriend then they both admired his body. One of them said something to Dante and he laughed. Somebody tapped me on the shoulder and asked me to move up. There was nobody ahead of me and I was holding up the line.

I gulped at the cold water, surprised at how thirsty I was. When I finished, I saw one of those girls give Dante a slip of paper that he put in his pocket. I stepped out of line and watched him and Chuckles head out the door. I willed him to look at me but he didn't. I wanted to follow him but that would have been way too much. Dante and Chuckles left the building.

I went into the locker room and ignored all the sissies giving me the eye. I took a long time getting my gym bag out of the locker. I sat on the bench while men of various shapes and sizes undressed around me. I unzipped my gym bag and stared at Sponge Bob.

3

The Black Woman and the Lois Lane Syndrome

I hate going to the office when I haven't been properly laid. It makes for a long day and turns me into more of an asshole than I already am. I'm one of those blacks in the office who talks back to the boss, you know, like Florence on *The Jeffersons*. Most of the time I get away with it, too. But I crossed a line with McGhee the last time and he's just looking for a reason to put me on the street. The only reason I haven't been fired already is because I out-sell all these jokers put together any day of the week. Even their good days are chump change to me. However, I still need to watch my step, and really, I should have been laid.

I nodded at the secretary who was on the phone and managed to slip through the security doors before she hung up. And thank God. That woman has the gift of Medusa: just one conversation and she'll turn you to stone. I ain't never seen nobody who can rattle on ad nauseam about being married and having kids. That's all that simple heifer talks about. I always shake my head at her and pretend to be listening but she hardly needs any encouragement. I guess it's because she's so isolated out there between the entrance to the building and the security door to the office. She really has no interaction with people unless they're passing through. That's when she begins her desperate need to communicate about the latest domestic drama in her Jane Q. Public life. The best thing about her is this: it's better when they do all the talking instead of asking all the questions.

Being on the down low in the office is a tricky thing. I don't want to get all deep about it because I'm not the type and you don't want to hear it; but there really is something, a philosophy in this country, that equates being successful with being married with children. I think somebody did a study on it. Women are always bitching and moaning about how society puts far too much pressure on them to be married and reproduce. Ironically, the number of mothers who are single by choice is on the increase. But men have it just as bad as women do. If you're not married with children, or better yet, have several girlfriends and several children out of wedlock, by the time you're 30, and you're a dude, then people just assume you're gay.

I'm 35.

That means, in the presence of the straight folks who run this world, I need to be either be talking about a woman, or be seen with a woman, most of the god damn time. I have to make a joke about Tyra Banks's titties. Something about coming on them. The cruder the better. Even the Christians laugh at that one. I have to look at the new piece of female ass passing by and make a comment about it to chuckling men. Every now and then I have to drag Kim, or some new girl who's trying to get married, to a Christmas party, or a company picnic. I have to tell the fellas how she is in bed, which isn't too hard since I still sleep with females. Just not as much as I used to. I have to allow myself to be set up by men's wives who are determined to find me a good woman. Then, I have to do something horrible to the blind date so that she will be the one who leaves me. Never the other way around. If I leave her then it might look suspicious. Why am I leaving a beautiful woman like that? But if she catches me with another woman, or counts the condoms and they come up short, or we have sex and I don't call her back like I said I would, thus breaking one of her unforgivable rules, then *she's* the one who tells the wife what a dog I am, who tells the husband, who tells the fellas, and that's how I maintain respect. After all, better a dog than a fag.

I'm pretty good at it, too. I'm a genius, in fact. I always get irritated when the media makes a big deal about a straight actor playing gay. Greg Kinnear got an Oscar nomination a while back for all that nancy-boy over acting he did in *As Good As It Gets*. If that was as good as it got then he wouldn't last a day in my world. The Rock got a whole lot of attention for playing a fag in the *Get Shorty* sequel. Now first of all, I'm not gonna talk too bad about The Rock because I want to bone him just like everybody else. Second of all, what's the big deal? It's not like he had to fall in love with a man or something, like they did in *Brokeback Mountain*, so what he was doing wasn't all that challenging. The Rock basically made a few homo jokes about fashion in the movie. So what? I adore the taste of dick in my mouth and I don't give a damn what you're wearing. The Rock, or Heath Ledger, or Tom Hanks, or Will Smith, or any supposedly straight actor playing a fag has never impressed me because I play a role every goddamn day and ain't got an award for shit.

Big deal if a straight actor is playing gay. Like they're playing an alien or something. Like it's so unusual to fake sexual orientation. Like it's so fucking rare. Please. Every day, in every way, somebody gay is fooling your ass. And the reason it's so easy to do is a matter of mental judo. We just use the forward motion of your own mind against you.

The thing that *Essence* and *Sister 2 Sister* forgot to tell you when they were using the fear of faggots to sell magazines is this: if black women didn't expect every sissy in the world to act like their hairdresser, then they would be able to see more clearly who's gay and who isn't. If women weren't so desperate to get married and have babies, like all their friends, then they wouldn't be so easy to fool. And don't start that misogyny stuff with me. Hell. Gay men, in general, don't hate women. The straight men who beat your ass, sleep with your friends, and don't pay child support hate women. Naw, faggots just want to be left the hell alone. That's our gay agenda. And since there is nothing more determined than a black bitch with a wet pussy, we have to sleep with you in the short run, to get the peace we want for the long run. Or at least as long as peace can last. Because if we don't fuck you, you'll tell everybody we're gay. And we can't have that, now can we? So we fuck you.

The thing that *Essence* will never tell you, because that's a magazine dedicated to making you feel good about your bullshit, is this: you're easy to fool because you don't want to see the truth. And the ones who think they're too smart to be fooled are the easiest targets of all. A straight man will tell you that much if you catch him being honest. It's no trick to fool a dumb woman. The educated woman thinks you should automatically want her and believes herself too hip to be played.

Because of that arrogance she's the first to fall. She doesn't, for one minute, even consider the fact that a masculine man would want a man instead of her. I call it The Black Woman and The Lois Lane Syndrome. I say… The Black Woman… and the Lois Lane Syndrome.

People think Lois Lane is stupid because she can't see that Clark Kent is Superman. She isn't. She's an able career woman who is the top reporter for a major metropolitan newspaper. Dumb women don't become top reporters for major metropolitan newspapers. The dumbest thing about Lois is that she's always managing to fall out of a tall building. I mean, my God, how many times can that happen? No, see, the reason Lois can't tell that Clark Kent is Superman is not because she's so dumb, or because a pair of glasses is such a brilliant disguise—but the reason she can't see the truth is because she's not *expecting* Superman to *be* anybody else. And Clark is just somebody she takes for granted.

Superman isn't like Batman. He doesn't wear a mask and isn't cloaked in mystery. He's always there when you need him to provide, like a husband or a boyfriend, and he looks damn good carrying you around. There he is to save the day. Making you feel special. Paying your rent. Supporting you in those big, strong arms that all your feminist girlfriends tell you that you don't need. And, honey? You love it. When Superman flies off into the sky after rescuing you from the latest villain in your life—an ex-boyfriend, an ex-husband, or low self-esteem—you never really know where he flies off to. Superman could live in the clouds, on the moon, or in Heaven for all you know. In fact, all you *do* know is that he's there when you need him and he's fine as hell.

And you believe what he tells you. After all, he's not wearing a mask like Spider-man or one of those freaks. Why would you think he has another side when you can see the face he shows you every single day? And hey, you're a real catch, girl. Especially when you're falling down all the time and he's there to solve all your problems. Or just hold you... like a decent man does. And he should be lucky to have you, too. I mean, why not? You're Lois Fucking Lane. A fine, educated woman with a good-ass job.

And Clark? Well, he's nobody really. Clark's not as exciting as Superman is. Just like that good man you keep around, as a backup, isn't as exciting as that unattainable man who sexes you right but is always out of reach. But good ole Clark. God love him. He'll always be around. He doesn't seem to have a lot of prospects so you know you can keep him on a string. He seems like he needs you and you like that. And Clark is just Clark. The ole stand by. The guy you've known for a long time. You're not expecting him to be anybody else either. Why would you be? All you can see is the man of your dreams on one hand, and the man who will always be around, on the other. They both fulfill your ego and expectations in different ways. He's a man and you're a woman, and that's the truth and justice of your American Way.

So when it turns out that Batman is stroking Superman up his sweet tender man hole, and has been for years, your little educated mind can't handle all that. Because that's the last thing you were looking for. Faggots dress like women. Faggots are not strong. Faggots are weak. Everybody knows that. Faggots are not heroes. You couldn't possibly be attracted to a sodomite. What would that say about you? And none of this is your fault, girl. All you were looking for—was what you wanted to see. And you never questioned the oddity of a grown man in his tights hanging around mysterious men who also wore tights. And you accepted the fact that he flew away at strange times because you knew he would be there again to catch you when you fell. And you never wondered why a dorky guy with glasses, who lived alone in his 30s, was apparently never interested in any other woman but you. No, you just chalked it up to being a catch, and hell, he couldn't do any better. That was just good ole Clark. And even though all your friends told you that something was up with that man... and even though, in retrospect, it was a little more obvious than a certain someone's ex... you can't blame yourself. No, no. It's his fault. And his alone. And you might have HIV, girl. So you enjoy the celebrity status of being a victim. Everybody'll feel real sorry for you. Because you're used to being rescued, honey.

Just like Lois Lane.

I know some of you ladies out there don't believe me. Ok, then. Don't shoot the messenger, baby, but apparently Stella Needs Her Glasses Back. Maybe she could borrow Clark's. Oh well. You know what they say: you can lead a horse to water but you can't make her think.

Aw, hell. Here comes McGhee.

"You're late." I'm not late and he knows it. I go to great lengths not to be late because they always expect us to be. But fine. I'll let him have this one.

"Sorry about that, McGhee. Won't happen again." He looked at me in skepticism, waiting for the sucker punch.

"Well, good. Let's go then." I followed his sunken ass down the hall to the board room. God, he's ugly. I've laid a few white boys in my time but I swear on the grave of Kunta Kinte they all looked like Nick Lachey. Not McGhee, though. McGhee looked like the type of plain vanilla boy who *People* magazine would name their Sexiest Man Alive. He was bald on top with those little Bozo poofs sticking out on the side. Just shave the whole thing already. He had a blonde mustache stained brown by I don't know what. He wore a cheap brown suit, with cheap brown socks, and a joke of a pair of cheap brown shoes. Everything about McGhee was cheap and brown. Oh-oh. So much for all that smack I was talking about not caring what people wear.

"You rooting for Alabama or Auburn?" he said. Like I gave a damn. The only reason I watched college football was to see thick men stuffed into tight white pants. But I kept up with the scores and ratings so I would have something to talk about with these dummies besides women. God, I hate straight people. I wish we could all just divide. Like amoebas.

"Auburn," I said. "You?"

"Oh, I'm not much into college ball." Then why bring it up, you dim motherfucker? God, I hate this stupid job. I wish I owned a gay porno studio. I could get blow jobs from 24-year-old actors and rake in the cash while they're doing it. You could just call me Spike Fag. Damn it, I really should have gotten laid or at least jacked off before I got here. Maybe I'm a sex addict or something, but isn't that kinda like being addicted to air? Anyway, McGhee opened the glass door to the bland board room and in we walked to the loser hall of fame.

There are six of us in all, including McGhee. Seated in the brown-noser position was Ted, a brother who made Al Roker look like a Crip. Now, I don't want to crack on Ted because he's smart or uses proper diction when he speaks. Lord knows we need more Urkels in the black community who act like they've got some sense. Niggas need to stop using ignorance as a measure of manhood. That's what a dick's for. But even though I wouldn't call Ted an Oreo, because that's just so high school, Ted's still not the kind of brother I would have warned we were running North back in the day. Ted always uses McGhee as his opinion barometer and then decides how he feels based on that. He's very proud of the fact that he lives in a gated community. Lord knows how he can afford it. Must be the wife's money. She's half white and he's proud of that, too. He never says that, of course, but it's worked its way into the conversation more than a few times.

Ted himself isn't bad looking. Dark skin, round face, non-offensive body. But there's nothing special about him either. He has a habit of correcting you and a tendency to stand too close when he talks. He wears glasses, that he uses a bit self consciously to gesture with, and he always talks a tad too loud like he's auditioning for community theatre. In fact, Ted has a habit of talking a lot, especially when the rest of us are manning the phones, because Ted's a lousy salesman. He couldn't sell a boat at Katrina. "No thanks, brother. We'll wait for the next one." This job pays a salary, in addition to commission, and that's a good thing for these fools because they can't fly without a net.

Like Tammy. She's one of those thick-ankle gospel sisters who wears too much makeup and works religion into the conversation at unnatural times. You know the type. Like if you say,

"How you doing, Tammy?"

She'll say, "Blessed! And you?" How the hell am I supposed to respond to that?

"Oh, I'm enlightened. Thanks for asking." Honey, please. Just say "fine" and move the hell on. She's always asking me to go to church with her. Like that's exactly how I want to spend my Sundays. Squeezed into a hot pew next to her chunky ass. Hell, I'm just getting home on Sunday from being out all night.

She oughta try it sometime. She might find a man. Because she's always saying stuff like, "I keep praying and praying for the Lord to send me a good man."

"You ever go out?" I say.

"Child, naw. Ain't nothing out there. I'm too old for that carnival."

"Well, what about your church?" I say. Not really caring but just something to say before the elevator comes.

"Oh, sure, I meet the brothers in Christ in the volunteer committees and that type thing. But they don't ever ask me out, child. Too much woman for them I guess." Then she laughs that forced, noisy, fat-girl chuckle that all of them have.

"Well," I say, "You ever think about talking to them first?"

"Oh naw, child," she says with horror in her voice. "My mama ain't raise no hos." Her mama ain't raised no brides either. Apparently, Jesus is supposed to gift wrap a man and just put him under her Christmas tree. Tammy likes to talk about the power of prayer and the gifts of the anointed. She sometimes asks to lead the sales group in prayer, and we always say yes, with a bit of discomfort, mainly not to look bad, and to just shut her up. But God must really hate Tammy 'cause that bitch can't sell fresh sheets at a Klan rally. Maybe she's not praying hard enough. I don't know. Every now and then, you'll hear

Tammy slam down her phone, after the latest failure to close, and say something like, "Oooh, the devil is busy in here today." It ain't the devil, cupcake. It's you. You in the wrong profession, sweetie. But I just might surprise Tammy and meet her one Sunday morning. After all, every faggot knows, if you want to find a good man, you meet him in church. Usually in the gospel choir, which is the religious queer equivalent to working on Broadway. On the subject of church, though, I think somebody needs to pray for poor Gary.

Gary is the prince of all geeks without the neo-geek charm. He's a nice enough kid. Jewish, I think, I'm not really sure. I don't go around dividing white folks up into groups like that but he's got something, Italian or something, in him. He's not Ambercrombie white, I know that much. I actually like Gary, though. He's a lot of fun to talk to. I could honestly say he's the only person in this place I look forward to seeing. That is, if you held a gun up to my head and made me choose. But God damn. Poor Gary's face is so fucked up with acne he should probably get handicapped parking. It's hard to look at. It really is. There's not a place on his face you can focus on that isn't layered and packed with whiteheads and red bumps. All of it looking like it could spurt at any minute if he opened his mouth too wide. He's truly ruined. I'm telling you that right now. And I never eat with this fool. Are you kidding me? Somebody needs to put him on one of those Save the Children commercials so his face can get a sponsor or something. It's bad. Black greasy hair. Weak chin. Yellow teeth. You would think there was somebody in his family, or a friend perhaps, who could take him aside and say, "Look, brother. This is a toothbrush. And this? Well, this is Clearasil. Use them wisely. They have great power." It's a shame. It really is. I know he never gets laid. I just bet he don't. But Gary's sweet, though. And funny. Maybe that can work for him one day. Who knows? Poor bastard. Couldn't sell vagina at a lesbian farm.

And then there's Charles. Please don't get me started on that one. He's always going on about America this and immigration that. I think he masturbates to *The O'Reilly Factor*. Ted's always grinning in Charles's face and doesn't realize that man doesn't like him at all. Any white man who complains about immigration is just one Heineken away from saying something about niggers. But Charles knows not to mess with me. One day he came into the office and said, "It's a shame about all the people those black guys killed, huh?"

You remember when that fine brother went crazy and started using human beings for target practice? Had that cute little piece of jailbait with him? Damn shame. Of course it is. But everytime something horrible happens in the news, and a black person is involved, I can always count on Charles to bring it up. I got to the place where I would listen to the lead-in on *CNN* and pray, "Please, don't let him be black." Hell, I almost quit a job during the O. J. trial. So anyway, Charles says shame and I knew where he was going with this so I said, "And so unusual, too."

"Unusual how?"

"Well you know, most serial killers are usually white. Even white folks admit that."

"Hm." Then he stirred his coffee with ten packs of low-calorie sweetener before he found the nerve to say, "I don't think it really matters, though. Do you?"

"Does what matter?"

"Who's black and who's white. I mean why make it racial? I mean more black people commit more crimes that whites. Now that's just statistics. Can't argue with facts."

"Maybe," I said. "But the majority of crimes that involve killing a whole bunch of people at one time are done by Caucasians. I guess white folks are just more efficient."

"Well now you're trying to be funny, man. Save that crap for McGhee. I thought we were buds." Buds? Do people still say that?

"Oh, we're cool, Charles."

"Good." He extended his hand and I shook it and that's when he made all these crazy grips on my hand. I finally realized he was trying to do a "black" handshake.

"Hey, look at that," I said. "Somebody's been watching *BET.*" Tammy laughed and Charles's face got red. I'm so glad that can't happen to me. Imagine having a sign hanging around your neck telling the world when you got embarrassed. Spare me.

Another time we were in the break room, just me and Charles, and a commercial for *Ellen* came on. I forget the particulars but whatever she said made me laugh. Charles shook his head and said, "It's something how she made everybody forget about that, huh?"

"Forget about what?"

"That she's a sodomite. I mean, come on. She's a sodomite. But then, one Disney movie and a talk show later, and we're running around pretending she's normal. Can you believe that?"

"Yeah, that's fucked up. She ain't found the right dick yet, that's all." Charles laughed and shook my hand, and the next thing I knew, I was giving him the *BET* handshake. I couldn't believe I did that. It just happened before I knew it. Charles smiled, as if we accomplished something, as if we had bonded. He left me in the break room and I stared at the floor for a long time while the tv blared on. I just stared at the floor. I don't know why.

I hated Charles most of all after that.

So anyway, I plopped into my chair while McGhee took the podium. The so-called salesmen all nodded at me and I nodded back at them. Charles gave me a thumbs-up sign.

"Good weekend?" he said.

"Oh, yeah."

"Oh, brother. You even remember their names?"

"I don't know. She couldn't talk with her mouth full." The fellas laughed and Tammy made a point of clearing her throat.

"Excuse me, gentleman, there is a lady present," she said.

"Well tell her we're all out of gentlemen," Gary said. We all laughed while Tammy threw a wad of paper at Gary.

"All right everybody, settle down," said McGhee. "The front office says our numbers are down again and it's a big problem this time." They all tensed up while I read the newspaper. I more than pulled my weight around here and shouldn't even be at this meeting. "You want to pay attention?" McGhee said to me. "This is important." I fought my natural urge to say something cute since I needed this job. There ain't nothing more tragic than a fag with no money. "Front office says we got sixty days to turn our department around or they're gonna let us go."

"Us?" I said. I didn't know my voice could get that high. "All of us?"

They looked at me funny. "Of course," said McGhee. "What'd you expect?"

I expect to keep my job since I'm the only one here who's good at it. That's what I should have said but I didn't.

"Lord Jesus, what we gonna do?" Tammy said.

"We're going to have a contest," said McGhee. "As motivation." Motivation? Motivation is for people who aren't good at what they do. It's a mind game for weaklings who can't get it up when the camera is on them. I don't need it. "The first prize is a new car." Ok, now I'm motivated.

"What kind of car?" said Charles. Why should he care? He couldn't sell insurance to a suicide bomber.

"A new Jaguar. Fully loaded, right off the lot."

"Oh, but the ladies gonna love me in that," I said. "Now, McGhee, isn't this a little unfair? Everybody knows I'm gonna win." They all booed and Gary shot me the bird.

"I wouldn't be too sure about that," Ted said. "You check the board lately? I'm catching up to you."

"Keep your fantasies to yourself, brother." I winked at Tammy.

"I'm serious," he said. "Check the board."

"Brother, the first step is admitting you have a problem."

"All right," said McGhee. "Pipe down. Now listen up." McGhee loved these lame meetings where he could butch up and act all Trump for a minute. Man. A new car. I can't wait to pull up in Griffith Park in my brand new ride on a Sunday afternoon so all the boys can see me before we cram into the club. Yeah. I could live with that. There's nothing wrong with the car I've got, so I could sell it for even more paper. All right. Maybe this won't be such a bad day after all. "We will be working in teams." Aw hell. "Now the first team will be—"

"Wait a minute," I said. I felt myself panic. "How could one of us win a new car if we work in teams?"

"They'll just give us two cars. Now stop interrupting me, will you? Geez!" I'm about one second from grabbing McGhee by those Bozo poofs and ramming my knee in his nose. Damn it! I hate working in teams. Did Beyoncé need a team? Did Cher need a team? Did Terrell Owens need a fucking team? Honey, I work alone! "Now the first team will be..." Please don't let me get Tammy or Ted. Please let me get Gary. Let me get Gary. "Gary and..." Come on, come on. "Gary and Charles." Damn it! Please don't let me get Tammy. Don't let me get Tammy. Let me get Ted. "Ted, you'll partner with me." Damn!

"Looking forward to it, boss," Ted said.

"Looks like it's you and me, boyfriend," Tammy said with that boisterous laugh of hers.

"All right!" I said. I gave her a smile with an enthusiastic high five. I can't stand this stupid job. Where's a 24-year-old porn star when you need him?

4

Parks & Recreation

God, I love the park. I don't know what it is about faggots and parks but we go together like Pride festivals and free AIDS testing. And Griffith Park is all that and more. I've seen the Griffith Park Observatory in the movies a dozen times and didn't even know what I was looking at. Then when I moved out here I was like, "Oh, that's the tower Demi Moore jumped out of, holding her golden guns, when Charlie's Angels discovered she was evil." I love Demi Moore. You know you're a star when you can cry one tear out of one eyeball and still look pretty when you're doing it. You go, Demi. Still fine in your forties with a handsome young man on a string. Bitch, I wanna be you when I grow up.

Anyway, I love having sex in the park and the possibility of getting caught is a thrill unless it actually happens. If you get a Damron Guide—that's a travel guide you can buy on Amazon that tells you where the gay bars are in each state—they'll also tell you which parks to go to. I don't go anywhere without my Damron. They include a AYOR (at your own risk) warning, but that's common sense for any park. They also warn you about where the undercover cops like to frequent. So watch out, fellas. Policemen get Damron Guides, too.

Always ask, "Are you a cop?" Even if you're not selling yourself. Just don't take it for granted that you're being approached because you're so fine. That's how they got George Michael. For some reason, cops have to tell you the truth if you ask them. That seems so silly to me. What's the point of being undercover if you have to tell the truth? That would be like me telling the truth if somebody asked me if I was gay. Come on. The answer is always no. But I don't know why cops have to tell you the truth. Something about entrapment. Who cares? That's the way it is and that's good for us homos. 'Cause there ain't nothing more embarrassing than being caught by the cops when you're a faggot in the park and you're on the down low. Nothing. That's some life-ending, career-ending, family-ending drama, and baby, you can't handle it. So hide and hide well. You know they publish those arrests in the newspaper, right? I knew this brother who got caught like that one time.

It was when I lived in Atlanta during the early '90s. I was in a relationship at the time with this Scorpio who made love like he taught it in college. I was so cute back then. You know. On the inside. Ah, I remember it like it was on tv last night. I had it all planned out. I was just going to go to Atlanta to get this gay stuff out of my system but then I fell in love. It was my first and last relationship.

This story begins in Piedmont Park, located in the heart of Midtown, the gayest section per capita in Atlanta. I had only one best friend in my lifetime and his name was Jesse Chuma. Everybody else I met in Atlanta were one-night stands, who I wouldn't acknowledge if I saw them in the gym the next day, or straight acquaintances who I was never myself around. Jesse was my only friend; the only one who knew me. I was young, just 23 years old, and paranoid to the extreme. I had just moved to College Park, and got turned out by the Scorpio, so I really didn't know that much. I think I was functionally crazy. Here I was living with this guy, while keeping it a secret from my family. I even supported us both through my job at Kaiser Permanente. Yeah, I was pretty stupid, all right. And nervous, always nervous. I didn't know how to be by myself when my lover wasn't there and I developed a touch of agoraphobia. It took a great deal of effort for me to just get out of the house to go to work. Then, I'd page my lover's beeper over and over when I got home. He'd answer, if he felt like it, and I'd be so grateful for that. Oh yeah. I was sprung. Pains me to admit it but sucker was tattooed on my forehead.

--In my defense, I can only say I had no idea that being with a man would feel so good. The two or three times I had tried it before had ended with pain, or was interrupted by messiness, or had been hampered with clumsiness. When I was with the Scorpio it was a natural fit.

It was what God had built me for.

It blew my mind. I didn't know how to handle it and I had nobody to talk to. The Scorpio made me stop sleeping with women because he said that was cheating. I couldn't see how it possibly could be. He was a man and they were women. How could I be cheating with him unless I slept with another man? But he wasn't having it. He went out all the time but didn't want me to go anywhere. Truth be told, I liked it that way because I was so afraid of people seeing me at the club. Besides, going to the club on a regular basis would really mean I was gay. I know it doesn't make any sense but more people understand me than would care to admit.

I'd have the strangest dreams. There was this one, where I was naked on a stage, and a guard dressed in red would come take me away while an audience of hunchbacked men would point at me and laugh. The men were all beautiful except for these large grotesque humps dripping of puss. It was the only time I dreamt in color and I always woke up scared. I wouldn't tell my family about it and my lover was useless to talk to. I refused to go to a shrink because that would mean I was crazy. So I used to take these long languid walks in Piedmont Park.

Sometimes, I'd even tan when I was in the mood. I've never been one of those black folks who was scared of the sun. I loved feeling the sun rays soak into my back. I never burned and didn't mind getting blacker. There was this flat clearing, on top of a hill, right above where people walked their dogs. I would go to the top where I had a good view of 10th Street. Then I'd stretch out my towel, lie on my stomach, and tan. It always seemed like I was in desperate need of sunlight. I can't imagine why but, whenever I tanned, it was as if I was being fed.

I got a few strange looks from the white boys but I just kept my eyes closed and even felt comfortable enough to go to sleep out there. I must have been having my dream again that day. I heard a voice so muffled that it sounded like it was coming through water. I knew I was dreaming but I couldn't wake up. Somebody shook me and I sat straight up and hollered. This guy was kneeling down beside me with look of deep concern. I draped the towel around me and wiped my corner of my mouth. The sun filtered past the IBM building. The light slanted through the oaks and the weeping willows and surrounded the form of Jesse Chuma.

Damn he was black. I know I said I didn't mind getting blacker but Jesse was the kind of black that wasn't from around here.

"You all right?" he said. "You be screaming like a mad man for true." He was from Zimbabwe. He helped me to my feet and laughed at the erection that only sleep could bring. I watched him laugh and didn't feel embarrassed so I laughed, too. I put my shirt on and we walked around the park to become instant friends. Neither of us was each other's type so there was no sexual tension. Neither was intimidated by the other so there was no need to impress. We just walked and talked, looking at the mothers with strollers, the homeless people on the benches, and the school kids running out of Grady High.

He hadn't been in Atlanta that long himself so we had that in common. He too loved a man who was great in bed but treated him like nothing. We talked about his mother, who was a shopkeeper, and his father, who was a laborer, and what they expected of him: marriage and good grades from his classes at Moorehouse. "They don't be tolerating the homosexual over there ya know. That a bad thing, man."

"They don't tolerate it over here either," I said.

"But they kill ya for it over there, man."

"They'll kill you for it over here, too. It's no different."

"It plenty different. Typical spoiled Yankee ya are. Not knowing how good ya have it." We sat on the pier and watched the ducks follow each other in perfect rows. Then, like all people in fucked-up relationships, we gave each other advice.

"You should leave him," I said.

"Yeah, but he know me so good and I love him so. We make a fit. See what I mean?" He told me how Cal, that was his name, had taken care of him in bad times and he felt it would be an act of betrayal to walk out on him now. Cal also paid the rent. Money keeps more bad relationships together than unwanted pregnancies.

"You a good-looking boy for true," he said. "You could have anybody you want to, no?"

"No. I don't want nobody else." I didn't think anybody else could make me feel that good. Time would prove me wrong, over and over again, but most 23-year-olds don't think about the future unless they plan on running for office one day.

Jesse and I began to hang out in spite of our various lovers' suspicions. People who cheat all the time can't conceive of platonic friendships. But I wouldn't give Jesse up and he held on to me as well. One day, I went to visit him in his apartment in Stone Mountain.

That's when I met Cal. When I first saw him, I reasoned that he must have been hung because there wasn't anything special about him on the surface. He was short with big, yellow frog eyes. He seemed friendly enough. I made a point of inviting him along to Taco Cabana in order to reassure him there was nothing funny was going on. He declined and Jesse went on to use the bathroom before we left. Cal and I were left alone, talking about the type of things people with nothing in common talk about, and that's when he started rubbing himself. I kept talking as if nothing was happening because I really didn't know what else to do. That's the type of thing sexual predators count on: the element of surprise and the victim's need for normalcy.

"Jesse! Hurry up!" I said.

"Hold your horses, ya spoiled Yankee bastard!" Cal winked at me and took it out. I was right. It was the only remarkable thing about him. God must have endowed a short fella like that to make sure tall folks didn't rule the planet unchallenged. He rubbed the head and made it slick and that's when I got hard myself. I forced myself to look away and was ashamed at my involuntary reaction. I heard him slap it in his hand trying to get me to look but I wouldn't. He kept talking while I heard water run in the bathroom. He chatted about the weather, about the traffic, about the game. When the water stopped running, he tucked it back in, and pulled his big t-shirt down over his pants. Jesse came out of the bathroom and Cal gave him some money while staying seated.

"What the matter with ya?" Jesse said to me. "Ya look like ya seen a haint."

"I'm just hungry, man. Let's go, already."

"Calm yaself, ya spoiled Yankee bastard." We got in my car and I never told Jesse because I didn't think he could handle it. I understood how much it would hurt him if he couldn't have this man. Even if it was Cal.

One day, Jesse called me, crying up a storm, and said this time he had had enough. We had been friends for almost a year so I didn't really pay that any mind since he said it once a month. Speaking of repetition, the Scorpio and I had fallen out again, too. It was a true Gays of Our Lives moment complete with the throwing of glasses and the calling of cops. This meant I would be single again for about two whole weeks before I let him move back in. Anyway, Jesse was hysterical, which was uncharacteristic, and he wanted me to meet him in Piedmont Park.

I drove to Midtown from Marietta worried he might tell me he knew what happened between me and Cal. His friendship meant so much and I couldn't picture myself without him. However, when I found Jesse on the pier, he wasn't tripping about me but rather Cal's latest escapade with a bartender from Loretta's, the main black, gay club back then.

"I can't take it no more, man," he said. "I give this fella all I am. I die for this man if I could. And he treat me like dirt." I wanted to invite him to crash with me for a few days but I was worried what the Scorpio would think if he dropped by unexpectedly. I hate to admit that. It really didn't matter because, just as I thought, Jesse wasn't ready to leave Cal yet. "But I'm gonna have my fun, too. Show him what it feel like."

That's when Jesse told me about the trail.

Apparently, there was this trail in the park that gay men went to where they could have sex with each other in the woods. I'd never heard of such a thing before. "How long has it been there? Who made it?"

"How should I know?"

"But how can people do that in broad daylight and not get caught?"

"Let's find out." He stared at me with a challenge in his eyes.

"Uh, look, Jesse. Let's just stay friends, dude." Jesse laughed so hard I turned around to see who was looking.

"Like I want ya, ya arrogant Yankee bastard. 'Sides, we both be liking the meat too much to satisfy each other." He had that right. In those days, I was strictly a bottom. The Scorpio only let me fuck him on Mardi Gras and my birthday. It's funny how gay men get hung up on stuff like that. In the eyes of straight folks we're all a bunch of fags but gay men like to play this game where they grade each other on their latent heterosexuality, based on whether they give or receive. The guys who are tops congratulate themselves for not being bottoms because being a bottom would mean they were really and truly gay. At least as a top they have something in common with the straight men who despised them. It's pathetic really. Besides, being the bottom is no position of weakness.

Sure, in the olden days, the warriors would rape the men of the tribes they conquered, not necessarily because they were gay, but because they wanted to turn the men into women. Being a woman was one step up from a donkey back then. To turn someone into the woman meant you owned them. You conquered them. They were your property. I guess that's why men, both gay and straight, say during sex: "Whose is this?" They really need to know. They have to know that they're in charge and the bottom understands and agrees with that. All is not fair in love and war but all's the same in love and war. The mechanics and mindset of conquering a body is no different from conquering a nation. You move in. You move out. You invade. You top.

But that was back then, when people thought the world was flat and twins were a sign of the devil. Today, being the bottom means to be the thing desired. To be the thing desired means to be in the seat of power. This throne I'm sitting on will make men come to attention and compete to have my prize. To be inside my kingdom. They'll turn their backs on their women and their God for just a taste of that which is mine. And I decide whether they're worthy or not to be on top. I rule who comes inside. I make the decision to share myself and don't feel debased by the action. Face it: It takes a real man to get fucked up the ass.

It took me a while to get to this point. Back then I was just another faggot in Piedmont Park. And my best friend Jesse thought the best way to retrieve his self esteem would be to have sex with a stranger in the woods. And I agreed with him. God help me, I agreed with him. I was still too paranoid about going to the trail in daylight. So we decided, in the glory of our twenty-something-year-old wisdom, that the safest thing to do would be to enter the park at night.

I picked him up at his place a couple of hours after it got dark. Cal greeted me at the door and gave me a long hug where he pressed himself against me. I pushed him away roughly and that's when Jesse walked in from the bathroom. I couldn't tell if he saw us or not.

"Let's go, Yankee."

"Where yall going?" Cal said.

"We going out," said Jesse.

"Out where?" Jesse ushered me on out and closed the door behind him. We could hear Cal curse and then laugh as we left. We got in my orange Volkswagen and hit the road. I was so nervous. We got to Piedmont and parked in front of Grady High School across the street.

"It's so dark," I said.

"Course it dark. It night."

"Maybe we should go to the club instead."

"Ya scared of the club and ya know it."

"Look at that!"

"What?"

We saw some figures walk swiftly across the street while carefully looking both ways. There was a brief glimpse of them in the streetlight before they were swallowed up by black.

"Hurry up," Jesse said. He hopped out of the car and slammed the door in his excitement.

"Don't break my door off," I complained.

"Calm ya self. Talking 'bout a door. Where I come from, some people don't even have doors." Every time Jesse talked about Zimbabwe it sounded one step away from *Mad Max Thunderdome*. I half expected him to tell me he was beaten daily with sugar canes. I never cared about geography so I never knew if he was making it up or not. What I did know is he was eager to march into that park and I ran to catch up with his wide strides.

We came to the top of the embankment and struggled not to slide down the wet grass while we made our way down the hill. We held onto each other's forearms for support and giggled when we stumbled to the asphalt at the bottom. It sounds stupid to say the park looked different at night but it did. It was eerie to see something so familiar in the absence of light. The trees by the lake loomed like shadows waving back and forth in the breeze. The lake rippled with wavy reflections of the white moon. I was afraid. Jeffrey Dahmer picked up black gay men, brought them back to his apartment, and ate them. What in the hell were we doing out here? Even Jesse looked concerned. None of that African bravado anymore. He stared at the pier we usually sat on, which resembled a plank stretched out into nothing.

"Listen," I said. "I don't like this. Let's just walk around the track one time, just to say we did, and then if you still want to cheat on Cal, we can just put our money together and get you a prostitute or something. I think they hang out over there behind the MARTA station."

"What ya mean, ya think? Ya know damn well where the hookers be, ya horny bastard." We heard voices coming from around the corner by the playground. "But fine. If ya just want to walk around one time then one time it be. Let's go." Like he was doing me a favor.

We began a brisk walk around the track, with our hands in our pockets, and huddled so close together our elbows kept bumping into each other.

"Watch ya self."

"Look where you're going." We rounded the bend by the playground and stopped at the same time. My God. There had to be at least fifty of them.

If those poor mothers who came here in daylight knew what was going down on those slides then they would never let little Timmy play there again. There was a swarm of them. That's what it looked like. A swarm of men, gathered in clumps, around the playground in different spots. We walked forward, not saying a word, trying to make out various shapes and outlines as our eyes adjusted to the dark.

I saw a pool of muddy water on the ground at the bottom of the slide. There was a group of teenagers and older men there; about four or five. One of them was either Hispanic or light skinned. The moonlight exposed the nicks and cuts of his freshly shaved head. He had his T-shirt pulled up above his stomach so he could stroke himself without obstruction. He had to be at least fourteen inches long. And young, too. Seventeen, eighteen, something like that.

This was back in the day when all the teenagers were first making the switch from tight jeans to baggies because tight blue jeans were becoming associated with gays. The only straight men who still wore tight jeans were country western singers and by the law of averages even some of them had to be gay. That's the one thing straight people never understood.

If you change the rules then we'll change the game. Straight boys wear baggy jeans and talk like gangsters? Fine. We'll wear baggy jeans and seduce the gangsters. Straight men get married to women? Fine. We'll marry women and bone the best man. Real men play sports? So do we. Just ask John Amaechi. And fuck Tim Hardaway. You can't stop us or kill us. Not all of us, anyway. And if we don't want you to... you won't find us either. We're everywhere. And we're not going anywhere just because you want us to.

Jesse elbowed me, to get my attention, and nodded toward the man getting worn out on the slide. This skinny brother was all nude and lay on top of his clothes that he had spread out for a cushion. One man had him by his left leg, another man had him by his right leg, and they stretched him open like a wish bone. All the while, a third big, broad man, who I had seen on the street before begging for change, was punking the skinny man out. A crowd was attracted to the howls of the skinny one. Jesse and I were jostled aside while people pushed closer to the action; crouching to see the point of penetration. The crowd was so silent but every now and then someone would grunt in approval and a strange man behind me kept saying under his breath, "That's the real shit right there. Yeah." I turned around and he was looking at me. That gave me the creeps so I got on Jesse's other side. He asked Jesse, "Oh, that's yours right there?"

53

Referring to me. I elbowed Jesse and he nodded in the affirmative. But I think the stranger saw me give Jesse the nudge because he gave me a dirty look before he moved on.

The skinny one getting poked on the slide was having himself a time. He was making those sounds that Eddie Murphy made in *Raw* when he said that's what a woman sounds like when the pipe gets good to her. And I guess Eddie Murphy would know. My heart was beating so fast and it was hard to see what the participants were actually doing. Every now and then someone would flick their lighter or let their cell phone glow so they could get a better look.

The moon was half swallowed by clouds and I checked out the rest of the playground to distract myself from my nervous stomach. I saw a studious man, who looked like he could be somebody's dad, and probably was, giving a blow job to a large thug rocking in a swing. At the top of a slide, the strange man who spoke to us earlier was gripping the rungs and letting himself get methodically pounded by the dude I recognized as the homeless man. Somebody touched my thigh and I brushed his hand away. This was freaking me out now.

Many of these guys didn't look clean and some of them smelled bad, too. How could anybody have sex without showering first? I guess they had other things, like survival, on their minds. Maybe sex in the park was part of their survival mode. I guess I could understand that. I still didn't like the way I was being stared at and it was way too dark. I heard groaning and shrieking and this was turning into Night of the Living Fags. It was definitely time to go. I turned around to tell Jesse we needed to go and that funny-talking jungle slut was nowhere to be seen.

Oh no. Oh no, he didn't. That National Geographic Cunt. I know that African Queen didn't just abandon me in the middle of this homeless orgy so he could have his revenge while I got raped by these zombies. I'm gonna kill Jesse. Hell, I got my own problems. I told him to leave Cal alone but can't nobody tell him nothing.

Well, the first thing to do was to find him. I should just leave him out here. That'd teach him. I gently made my way past the three-way on the merry-go-round and the transvestite getting ate out on the monkey bars. Then somebody called me.

I turned around and there was Cal in the doorway of the pool house. He was stroking the guy with the fourteen inches making his hard meat bounce like a pole about to break. Cal spanked the boy's bottom and waved me over. Obviously, he didn't know I was out here with Jesse.

At least, I didn't think so. Maybe he followed us? No. It's just one of those weird coincidences of being in the closet in an incestuous town like Atlanta.

The moon broke free of its cloudy prison, granting me a clearer view of Cal deep in his conquest. I was so hard. Jesse forgive me. I was so damn hard.

"Freeze!" I heard somebody say. I didn't even know I could run that fast. Flood lights split the night and policemen stormed the playground. Sissies screamed like damsels in horror movies while cops moved in with guns. The camera crews were right behind them. I couldn't find Jesse anywhere. Then I fell and a stampede of men tripped over me and pinned my face in the mud.

"What are you doing in the park this time of night?" The reporter said. She was talking to a handcuffed man, whose pants were still down, and he ducked his face so nobody would see him. That wouldn't fool anybody who really knew him, though. I tried to get out from under the bodies but more people kept falling on our pile. I punched the man on top of me and he punched me back hard in the face. He finally pushed the person off on top of him. He scrambled off me but stepped on my ankle when he ran away. I heard dogs barking.

"This is a raid! Everybody put your hands on top of your head and stay where you are!" There was no way I could let the approaching cameras see me. The people I worked with at Kaiser watched the news religiously. I jumped up but the pain grounded me. I wasn't going to make it. Once more, I tried to stand and again my ankle brought me down.

"Does your wife know you're out here, Councilman?" The reporter said. I recognized that guy with the salt-and-pepper hair as an Atlanta city councilman. I had heard some rumors about him but never paid them any attention. You hear rumors about everybody. Hell, I even heard Jesus was gay.

I felt a hand on my shoulder and was relieved to see Jesse. He saw me clutch my ankle and assessed the situation with ease. He swatted people out of the way, put my arm around his neck, and lifted me up. "Freeze! Get on the ground!" We ran, of course, or rather Jesse ran and I hobbled to next to him as fast as I could. I heard somebody chasing us. "Put your friend down and drop to the ground!" We heard a gunshot and somebody hollered. I couldn't believe they would shoot us just for being in the park at night but stranger things have happened. Then, we were tackled and I screamed as the pain from my foot hit me. I grabbed my ankle and rolled on the ground while Jesse tussled with a big, white cop. "Don't make me shoot you, son!"

"Run!" Jesse said. I hopped on one leg up the hill and heard them scuffle behind me. I heard more gunshots and jumped a little faster, running out of breath. I thought I could hear Jesse say something like *take it easy, man* and maybe I heard the cop say *put your hands behind your back.* I don't know.

I ran into traffic and a black Expedition almost hit me. The driver leaned on the horn and somebody rolled down the window. "Watch where the fuck you going, motherfucker!" The SUV was full of people. Rap music and smoke poured out of the window. "Get the fuck out the way, nigga! You trying to get hit?" I tried to cross the street but the traffic wouldn't let up. Atlanta isn't like New York. They don't play that pedestrian-has-the-right-of-way stuff down South. My ankle was killing me and that stupid driver kept honking his horn.

I heard a woman scream and this fat, naked brother ran past me into the street. Cars screeched to a halt and the big bastard just kept on booking with his bare feet patting the pavement. The people in the Expedition laughed and hooted and more people in traffic honked their horns. A multitude of men, some half clothed, ran out of Piedmont and into the street. Somebody in the vehicle said, "Look at all them faggots running out the park!" I looked past the headlights and could dimly see the driver's face. "That must be one of 'em right there! There go one right there!"

Some woman's voice said, "Get that faggot!" The driver stepped on the gas and I jumped out of the way. I landed on my ankle and the pain brought me to my knees. More cars honked their horns and more people ran by me. I could still hear the voices of cops in the background.

I stood up to make my unsteady dash. As soon as one more car passed, I'd feel safe enough to run. I had now created a traffic jam on 10th but I wasn't agile enough to weave between cars like the other escapees were doing. Suddenly, this ghetto ass, Sha-Nay-Nay bitch—I can still hear her roaring ignorant voice—said, "I hope all yall faggots die from AIDS!" And she hit me in the head with a bottle. Glass and something that smelled like gin shattered on the back of my skull and that brought me down again. She must have leaned out of the passenger side as they were driving by. I heard them laugh while they cruised down the street, not even in a hurry, honking the horn, and swerving towards other people running from the park. I touched the back of my head and looked at my hand. It was covered with blood and I was getting dizzy. *Please don't let me pass out in the street.* I hopped across the street, wishing I could kill that bitch with the power of thought. There was my car in front of Grady High where I left it. I fumbled into it and drove down the street, looking at blurred traffic lights as I went along.

I had to do something about all this blood. In my confused state, I had to be clean before I got home. Because what if the Scorpio made a surprise visit? How would I explain myself? I pulled over to a gas station but they didn't have public restrooms. I thought there might be one at the Wendy's across the street but it was full of people and I couldn't go in there like this. Then I remembered this restroom at the BP gas station on the corner of Piedmont and Ponce. I once let this fella give me a blow job in there and I knew I didn't have to ask for a key to get in.

I drove there while the blood soaked my back and forced myself not to cry. Would the stains wash out of the upholstery? How I would explain that if it wouldn't? For somebody who was injured, and could have been killed, I spent a lot of time worrying about what other people would think.

What would Jesse think about me leaving? What would the Scorpio think if he called and I wasn't home? What would Cal think of seeing me in the park? Would he think I was a regular there? Would anybody in those honking cars recognize me from the gym? Would the folks in the SUV brag about what they did to me? I wondered and worried about everybody except me.

I made it to the BP and felt lucky there weren't many people around. A lady pumped gas, with her kids in the car, and a few people were in the cashier's line inside. I pulled up next to the restroom door and looked around to make sure the woman at the pump wasn't watching. She said something to her kids and they locked the doors. I opened my trunk, and got out my gym bag, and prayed the bathroom door was unlocked. It was and I went inside.

Somebody had taken a big dump in the toilet and hadn't flushed the stool. I covered my nose and flushed the commode with my foot. I opened the door to let out the fumes but I didn't want the lady at the pump to think I was coming to mug her. So I closed the door, locked it, and breathed in the stench.

I looked at myself in the mirror for a long time and made a vow to always follow my instincts. I knew it was a bad idea to go to that park. I knew it and I went anyway. I got exactly what I deserved, including the bottle to my head. I should have listened. Gay people without instincts are dead. We have to be constantly on the lookout for danger. We have to be ever mindful of threats, just like animals in the wild, because we're screwed if we move too slow.

Slow means you're the appetizer. Slow means disaster. Slow means fired for being a dyke. We always have to be on the look out for the gossipy co-worker, the religious relative, or the school bully. Beware of the Chatty Cathy with a crush on you, or the teacher who can tell by looking at you, or the tv preachers with an ear to the White House, and sundry other predators.

I pulled as many of those rough, brown paper towels from the bathroom dispenser as I could ball up in my hand. I couldn't take the smell anymore and opened the door for fresh air. Whoever was in there before me was obviously in worse shape than I was. I peeped around the corner and didn't see anybody so I felt safe enough to leave the door cracked. I dabbed the back of my head and began the time-consuming process of cleaning my wound—wetting the towels, getting more towels, flushing the towels. I was in there for a while and the odor never subsided. I threw my bloody shirt in the trash and hoped I wouldn't need any stitches. Because I damn sure wasn't going to the hospital. How would I explain the injury? I've got a lumpy scar on the back of my head to this day. I told my barber I was in a car accident when he asked me about it. That was almost the truth. I got a fresh shirt out of my gym bag and stepped outside.

I made it home somehow. It reminded me of when I drank too much at Loretta's and the next thing I knew—I was home. Jesse told me that an angel must have driven my car. I was a lucky piece of fruit back then. I never really got hurt no matter how many stupid things I did.

The next morning, my pillow was smeared with blood and I had a headache so bad that it hurt my teeth. I showered and watched the red water swirl down the drain while I leaned on my good ankle. Afterwards, I put antibiotic gel on my head and took an aspirin. I put my ankle on ice and elevated it. I'd be all right. Now, I had to find Jesse.

I left a message on his cell phone and waited. Jesse always called back right away but this time he didn't. I phoned the jail to see if I could find out something new. "I'm calling to see if you've got a Jesse Chuma down there?" I watched television while the desk sergeant put me on hold to see if there was a story about it on the news. I checked out the paper and saw the headline in the Journal-Constitution: BOY'S NIGHT OUT, it said. The other sections of the paper fell to the floor and I trembled while I thumbing through to see if my picture was in there. I began reading the article but was interrupted when the desk sergeant came back to the phone. Jesse was there.

Later, I bailed Jesse out with some money I had in savings and told him not to worry about paying me back. I never said that to a man unless I was sleeping with him and back then I said it way too often. It was then I realized that I loved Jesse. Not romantic love but the kind of love where I cared for him as much as myself and I didn't feel pathetic about it. Jesse was quiet on the ride back home and I didn't dare tell him about Cal. We had a bigger problem: Jesse's picture, along with his name, made the paper.

I brought it along with me when I came to bail him out. If he didn't hear it from me he would have heard it from somebody else. He didn't read the article. He just stared at his picture; the shameful look in his eyes, his hands cuffed behind him, the blank expression of the cop. He folded the paper in his lap and stared out the passenger window while we stopped at the red light.

"Maybe I should take you back to my place," I said. I studied the license plate on the truck in front of me because I didn't know where else to look.

"It's over, man." His voice was dead tired. "It all be over now." I just kept memorizing those license plate numbers. I didn't ask him what it was like in jail, or if he had been raped, even though I wanted to know. I just told the same lie that everybody tells in those situations.

"It'll be all right," I said. He slowly turned his head and scolded me with disbelieving eyes. I couldn't handle returning his stare so I grabbed his hand instead. The truck in front me sped through the light and I rushed to catch up.

"You know how many cousins I got here in America, Yankee? And ya know how much they be talking to my people back home? You American gay boys really don't be understanding. Yes. You be having your problems here. I ain't stupid ya know. But it nothing like it be for the black man in Africa. It against the Bible here. So what? Some folks believe and some don't anyway. But it against the law back there. Family disassociate from the gay boys and they be left in the street back there. They kill for it back there. My people think it a white man disease. A white man sin. I never be able to look at my father again. My mother be disgraced. The boss at my job? He read the paper all the time. All the time every day. All right, ya say? No, boy. It ain't gonna be right no more." There was nothing I could say. I was about to turn on the radio when he said, "How the ankle?"

"It's fine." My ankle hurt like hell but I was scared to complain because he'd tell me in his country people didn't have ankles. "Thank you for helping me. I couldn't have made it out of there without you, man. I'm sorry I left."

"What a stupid thing to say. What be the point of us both in jail? I told ya to run now ,didn't I? Well didn't I?"

"Yeah."

"Well shut up about it then. Take me home."

"We need to find you a lawyer. Let's go back to my place. You could just chill while I look up some names in the book."

"I ain't bothering with that right now. Take me home, I say." I didn't look forward to seeing Cal but I didn't want to argue. Once Jesse had his mind made up about something that was pretty much it.

We pulled into his apartment complex, where he gave me the security card so I could swipe the gate from my window. We passed under the slow-raising arm and parked at the convenient spot right in front of his door. He seemed like he was ashamed to get out. Then, he dashed from the car to his apartment and I limped behind at my own slow pace. When I made it to the door, Jesse was slouched on the couch and looking at his picture in the paper. Cal wasn't there and that suited me fine.

"You want something to eat?" He said.

"I'll just order us a pizza. Where's the phone book? I'll call Papa John's."

"I don't want a pizza."

"Well, you gotta eat something."

"I don't gotta eat pizza. Sit down." I hobbled to the couch and kinda fell into it at an angle. "Put your feet up. Elevated. Always elevated." I put my foot up and we held hands and sat there for a minute. That's when Cal walked in with a basket of laundry. I snatched my hand away and Jesse looked at me strange.

"What the fuck yall doing in here?" Cal said.

"Mindin' our business," Jesse said.

"Oh, you trying to get smart?" He put the basket down and approached him. "You trying to get smart? Don't try to show out in front of your stuck-up friend 'cause I pay the rent up in here, little bitch." I hoped Cal wasn't gonna be a problem since I wasn't in shape to help no damn body. Jesse grabbed my hand and held it tighter when I tried to pull away.

"You see this man?" He said to Cal. "This man my friend. My brother. And we gonna be here for a while. If you try to hurt him, or put your hands on me again, I swear before God I kill you." Cal looked at Jesse with caution and covered his fear with a laugh. His laughter stopped when he saw the newspaper. He snatched it off the coffee table and stared at me.

"How come you didn't get caught too?" Cal said.

"Too?" said Jesse. "Wait a minute? How ya know the Yankee be in the park?" You could tell by the look on his face that Cal was the type of fella who should never play poker. "Well, yall left here together, didn't you?" Jesse rubbed the center of his brow in a slow circular motion. "Ok, then," he said after while. "Ok. I'll be right back." He went to the bathroom down the hall. "Make yourself useful and get him some ice."

"I'll get it," I said. I didn't want Cal anywhere near me.

"No," said Jesse. "Let him do something for somebody else for a change."

"For a change?" Cal said.

"Cal!" We watched Jesse shut his eyes tight, trying to keep it together. The upstairs neighbor banged on the ceiling. "Get the ice." Cal hissed his breath out through his teeth and sulked into the kitchen.

"We ain't through talking about this shit right here," said Cal. "You heard me?" Jesse went to the bathroom while Cal yanked open the freezer and snatched an ice tray out. He slammed the freezer, twisted the tray, and flung the ice into the sink. He scooped a couple of handfuls into a plastic bag. "Here you go." He dangled the bag high in the air.

"Just give me the bag, please."

"What you gonna give me for it?" I was burned out and let my head flop back on the couch. "You like what you saw last night?"

"You ain't worth shit. You know that? Jesse is in pain, man. Why don't you go see about your lover?

"I got enough dick for both of you," he whispered. "But you already know that, right?

"How do you know I won't tell Jesse. Huh? What makes you so damn sure about that?"

"Go ahead, then."

"Maybe I will, motherfucker. I ain't playing with you now."

"You a wolf, baby."

"Huh?"

"You a wolf. Take one to know one." He rubbed himself through his pants. "You a wolf. Don't try to fight it." I stared at this fool in disbelief.

"Why the hell does Jesse keep staying here?"

"I think you know." He took it out.

"Fuck you. Jesse!" He zipped himself back up while I hopped down the hall to the bathroom.

"Ok. Be cool, baby, be cool, now." He grabbed my arm and I pulled away. I knocked on the bathroom door.

"Jesse!"

"Ok, ok, man. I was just playing. Here go your ice."

"Go to hell. Jesse! I got something to tell you. Hurry up!" A chill went up my spine. I thought that was only a figure of speech but that's exactly how it happens. "Jesse!" Instinct. Too bad it didn't kick in sooner.

"What's the matter?"

"Call the police!" I put my ear against the door and could hear the water and the fan. "Jesse?" I banged on the door. I tried the doorknob and it had been unlocked all this time. I pushed it open.

5

The Will & Grace of God

I didn't go to the funeral because it was held in Zimbabwe. I couldn't afford to go and really what would I say when I got there? Who would I say I was? Now that the story was out about Jesse every man in his life was a suspect. The family now knew that Cal wasn't simply a roommate like Jesse told his cousins he was. They knew there was no girlfriend who he canceled an engagement with. They knew about the park. I couldn't go to the funeral. I just couldn't.

I wonder if they felt bad about it. I mean of course they felt bad but I wonder if they felt responsible about the fact that he considered death his only option. Probably not. Maybe. Hell, I don't know. You never know what another person is going through.

The Christians always get so self-righteous about suicide. To them, that's right up there with being a fag as the one way express to Hell. I prefer to think of it another way. I prefer to think that if there's a God then he's compassionate. And He figures that if Jesse was in enough pain to kill himself then the least He could do is to let him into Heaven. He'd already been through Hell on earth.

Fuck Christians.

I mean really. Do these people ever say anything that actually helps? I can't tell you the number of sissies I know who have long-term affairs with married men in the church. And some of these married men are pretty swishy themselves. For example, look at T. D. Jakes. That big greasy show boater is always talking against faggots but I've seen drag queens who act like more of man than he does. Just look at him. Especially when he really gets going with all that whooping and hollering, while those fools in the pews, who are making him rich, cheer his sweet ass on. That's when it peeps out. That's when I can tell. Now, I don't know nothing about T. D. Jakes for sure but I'm just saying. Look at Donnie McClurkin. He wants to blame being a fag on the devil. They all do. And now, presto chango, he's been healed of being gay. Right. That's like being healed of having brown eyes. I think he said was raped or something. I get so tired of straight people assuming I want to rape a child just because I'm gay. Pedophiles are sick. They have to take pills so they won't get hard around little boys. I, on the other hand, need a pill so I won't get hard around L. L. Cool J. The shrinks took faggots off their list of disorders a long time ago.

Because I'm not sick. I'm gay.

Look at Kirk Franklin. I mean come on. Look at him. Look at half of the Winnans gospel gang. Just open your goddamn eyes. Look at Ted Haggard. He gets outed by his gay prostitute but after three weeks of prayer he's Just One Calorie All Sissy Free. This is what I mean by the Lois Lane Syndrome. Women don't want to see the truth and then they cry to Jesus if they get AIDS. Men don't want to see the truth either. Especially not the ones in the church. You know why? Because it's easier to pretend you're possessed by the devil rather than admit you want a dick up your ass.

It's a never-ending source of amusement to me how Christians like to pick and choose the parts of the Bible they feel like obeying. Isn't it funny how the greatest sinners in the world become biblically literate when it comes to homos? I mean, honestly, it's like it's the only part of the Bible they know. Never mind that people in these churches are committing adultery, stealing money, and abusing kids like it's a contest or something. When it comes to faggots every adulterer, thief, abuser, and blasphemer is suddenly a biblical scholar.

Many will agree that Jesus Christ is the greatest figure of the Bible. Everything before him is a warm-up and everything after him is a letdown. Jesus says nothing against homos but he is vividly pointed against divorce. Yet millions of women, including female preachers, get divorces all the time. Today's woman is able to read the Bible and make value judgments based on equal rights and modern times. In fact, the modern woman can say with civilized confidence, relating to divorce, that Jesus ain't really talking about her. Her situation is different, they tried to make it work, and so on and so forth. So they get a much needed or much wanted divorce and no one, except the Church of Christ, thinks they're going to Hell for having the sense to get out of a relationship that isn't working.

On the other hand, when it comes to faggots, the Bible is to be taken literally. It's right there in black and white, the inspired word of De Lawd. How come sissies aren't afforded the same sliding scale of Christianity a person who wants a divorce gets? The justifications are the same, aren't they? The faggot's situation is different. The faggot tried to make the straight thing work. But the same instant scholars, who let female preachers slide with a get out of Hell free card, expect the homo to ignore modern times and follow the scriptures to the letter. Spare me.

I'm not against female preachers, though. A documentary on *A&E* said Mary Magdelene got a bum rap about being a whore and was likely one of the first female preachers with responsibilities among the twelve disciples. We've been hearing that Mary Magdelene was a whore for centuries. And it was wrong! What else in this Bible has been interpreted wrong that church niggers are taking as gospel?

Creflo Dollar sounds like a fool saying there's no such thing as being born gay even though scientific evidence says otherwise. Would he say there's no such thing as evolution? Bad example. I guess the devil scattered all these fossils around to confuse everybody. That's the problem with having a church the size of a football stadium. You start thinking you're a star. And stars believe their own bullshit.

The church niggers love to say that being a fag is an abomination because it says so right there in Leviticus. So what? It says a lot of shit in Leviticus that we don't do anymore. It says eating certain kinds of fish is an abomination, too. You think them church niggers are gonna boycott Red Lobster? I don't think so. And there's not a damn thing Bernice King can say to me about being a fag because it says so right there, in the same Bible she's condemning me with, that bitches shouldn't even be talking in a church.

So anyway, I'm not going to the funeral because I can't take being around a bunch of church niggers who hate faggots right now. I just can't. Especially not foreign ones. Poor Jesse.

Oh, yeah. I fucked Cal.

How does the expression go? Neither one of us meant for this thing to happen. The suicide created feelings of guilt and rage, and all those things that some shrink who isn't getting as much sex as I am, will be happy to go into great detail about. I went to a shrink once. Nice lady but she fucked me up more than I already was. That's when I started keeping a diary to *watch my thoughts*, she said. Watch my thoughts? It didn't work. Watching my thoughts didn't make anything happen, or make anything go away, or make anything better, or make anything easier. The Buddhists are full of shit, too. Introspection never got me anywhere.

I found Jesse hanging from a belt in the bathroom. He didn't even leave a note. That's another reason I didn't go to the funeral. He didn't think enough of me to say goodbye so why should I? I didn't know how to give CPR and I don't know if it would have mattered since the paramedic said his windpipe was crushed. And then he had shit on himself so now I'm covered with his shit because I'm trying to hold him up and he hanged himself in the nude. I don't know why he took his clothes off or what that was suppose to mean. Another reason why a note would have been helpful.

Cal was as useless as I was. We spent a good five minutes yelling instructions at each other before I finally called 911. So the cops come, and I'm stinking, and Jesse's name comes up as a recent arrest. And they know why. So now the cops and the paramedics are giving us these looks like, *what are you faggots up to in here?* And one of the cops finds some homemade porn of Jesse and Cal when he asked to look around. Cal could have, and should have, said no but he didn't want to look like he was up to something. It was all just a great big mess.

Cal came to my place about a week or so after it happened.

I was surprised to see him because I didn't realize he knew where I lived. I didn't like that but I let him in anyway. We sat there saying all the things people usually said in those situations.

"How could he do this?"

"I wonder if he felt any pain," I said.

"How come he couldn't tell me? Of all people he should have come to me."

"Did you say anything to him?" I asked.

"What do you mean?"

"Did you say anything to him. Anything more than usual? Maybe if you had been there for—"

"This ain't my fault."

"Yes, it is. You were a lousy boyfriend. Do you know how many times he cried over—"

"It wasn't my fault! I loved Jesse!"

"That's a lie. What were you doing in the park if you—"

"What were yall doing out there? Huh? Answer that! You take him out there?"

"Are you crazy? *He* took *me* out there."

"You a liar. That wasn't even Jesse's style. He didn't start this shit until you came along."

"I know you ain't trying to put this on—"

"We was fine until you came along. Then he had to act all bad because of you."

"What the hell are you—"

"Jesse was always trying to show out for you."

"Please. Ok? You made that boy feel like—"

"What about what he did to me? Huh?"

"Now it's his fault?"

"You damn right. Ain't my fault."

"It *is* your fault! If you had kept your dick in your pants—" He hit me. And then I tried to kill that fool. I picked up a lamp and swung at his head but he dodged and I hit him on the shoulder. The lamp broke and he tackled me. I was still vulnerable because of my ankle.

"Get off me!" I bit him. It's a bitch move, I know, but it got him off me long enough to roll on top of him where I punched his head, swinging wild over and over. My lungs were burning and my throat got dry. He covered up and I was mostly hitting his arms instead. He twisted around to his stomach and tried to get up but I pushed him back down to the floor again.

I kept hitting and screaming. I can't even remember what I said and then he cried. He cried and yelled for Jesse. I never saw a person cry like that before. His body shook, a convulsion really, and I didn't know what to do.

I told him to get up but I didn't get off him so he could. I yelled that it should have been him instead. He continued to cry and I grabbed him by the back of the neck and pushed his head to the floor.

"Shut up!" I became aroused. My voice dropped into my belly. "Shut up." And then it just happened like it was supposed to. I stretched out over him and covered his body like a blanket. My arms on his arms. My thighs on his thighs. He had such a juicy ass. I never noticed that before because I was always trying so hard not to look. But he did. I sank into his plump flesh and let myself grind there, breathing on his neck. His tears subsided and he let out a moan like a wounded man. His back rose and fell as his breath grew deeper and he returned my motion. Slowly, at first, then adjusting to my stroke. I knew I had him and could do anything I wanted to with him. The knowledge of my sexual power over another human being made me drunk and mean. I think that's the danger of the Tree of Knowledge. That's why God told Adam and Steve not to taste that fruit. Because once you understand what you can truly do to a man you always go too far.

I peeled his shirt off over his head and he stretched out his arms in compliance. I pulled him up, by his belt, to his hands and knees. I yanked down his shorts with impatience and slid my hand between his flesh, making him groan, watching his sweaty face. He found the courage to look at me and I put my thumb between his lips. He stared at me with wide eyes, almost looking silly, and sucked on my thumb because I told him to. I added my fingers, one at a time, until he tasted them all. I leaned in close and outlined his lips with my tongue.

Then he kissed me.

He kissed me right.

He kissed me the way a man kissed a man

When he knew he'd be spending the night.

Cal would end up spending the night there for a while. We didn't start dating or anything but we wanted to be around each other so that's just what we did. We'd been going through a mental dress rehearsal since the moment we met. Now that Jesse was gone there was no need to pretend. I never let myself feel bad about it because Jesse chose to leave and we chose to stay. I couldn't control this world that the straights were in charge of but I could damn sure carve out my territory. With Cal, I carved it all night long. No wonder Jesse would never leave this man. Cal was good at what he did, honey. And he was more than happy to give me a few lessons in the fine art of man pleasing because I was smart enough to ask.

I ended things with the Scorpio for good this time. He might have done it like he taught it in college but Cal had a doctorate in it. There was another reason I ended things with him. I never wanted a man to have that much power over me again. I never wanted to need a man that much, not even as a friend. I loved my friend and he left me. I loved my man and he played me. I was just as screwed up as everybody else on this mud ball floating through space. But as much as possible I wanted to win. I didn't want to be weak. I didn't want to be Jesse. Cal was right. I *am* a wolf. And being a wolf is better than being dead because there, but for the grace of God, go I.

6

Annie

Los Angeles is sometimes beautiful when I stroll down a hiking trail high in the mountains of Griffith Park. I can see a wide stretch of the city absent of fog. I usually saw the fog when I flew in from New York but here on the ground, in the midst of things, I rarely notice. Further down the trail, this Indonesian guy is trying to catch my eye. I've seen him in the club before. He's got a cleft lip but a sumptuous body. We fondled each other in the bathroom before but I never went all the way. I kept looking at his lip. I pride myself on my intellect but the truth is I'm pretty damn shallow. I love the appearance of things.

Today is Saturday. I'll busy myself with a lot of things to prepare for the hell I'm in for on Monday. The contest starts then and I'll have to think of some way to get Tammy up to par. So this weekend is a reward. I'll treat myself to carnal pleasures and recreational drugs. A few Long Island Ice Teas in the Circus maybe. Oh, wait a minute. I think that club goes straight on Saturday. Ok. I'll go to the Catch One or maybe call Tyrone. I'll hang out with the fellas at the bowling alley and this guy I met online knows about a sex party taking place in a warehouse in Los Feliz. Although, after all this activity, Monday will come and it doesn't change one thing.

I'm lonely.

Since I won't let myself have a boyfriend it's time to give Kim a call. I've been dodging her calls for a few weeks now. It only makes her want me more, it seems. It's been a while since I've seen Tyrone but Tyrone is unavailable on weekends. Tyrone has a family. Today, I'll go out with a pretty woman and be a part of the world.

I called her on my cell while the Indonesian masturbated behind a tree. Kim answered the phone on one ring. "Hey, you!" I hated that obnoxious perky greeting. It made me want to kick her in the face. I don't know why I didn't branch out and get more of a stable of women. I ran most of them off but I could still try a little harder. It's just that Kim is so convenient and always ready. I'd have to work too much with a new woman; at least, that's what I tell myself. I got hard watching the Indonesian while Kim prattled on. The mountain air, free of fog, bore my mind to an earlier time.

I was in love with a woman once. We met in college back in the days when I was trying to make it go away. You often hear that college is a time of experimentation in gay sex. I suppose, but for me it was an experiment in exorcism. I had already fought it down in junior high. I pretended it didn't happen once in high school with the principal's son. Now, it was getting stronger like a disease there was no remedy for or an opponent who was just too big. Now it came in my dreams, this need for men. When I watched television, I'd notice myself staring at Dwayne's behind on *What's Happening* more than Thelma's breasts on *Good Times*.

I didn't want to be different and I was afraid of going to Hell. Pain and fire forever and ever while demons tore my flesh. I mean honestly. Could you imagine? I could and I didn't want to go. So it was there in college where I went to find a woman so I wouldn't be different anymore.

I wouldn't have to look far. Annie was my lab partner in biology class and I'd often get in trouble with her because I'd always miss lab on Wednesdays. My grade affected hers so naturally she was pissed off when I wouldn't show up. I was a huge *All My Children* fan and it came on at noon. I'd be so wrapped up in the adventures of Erica Kane that I'd just plain forget about labs on Wednesdays. That alone should have told me something right there. Anyway, Annie was furious.

"Where have you been?" She asked one day when she cornered me in the quad.

"Oh. Hey, Annie."

"Uh-huh."

"I'm so sorry."

"You should be, darn it. This is my grade we're talking about here." She had that same curl in her hair that Michael Jackson's girlfriend had in the Thriller video. Her body was an elegant blend of athlete and model. "I'm up here," she said. She always caught me looking at her breasts. She wore a lot of *Charlie* and that smelled like my mother so I liked that; a smell reminiscent of home. "How come you never make it to labs? Do you, like, have a girlfriend or something? Because you can just tell her that you'll have to see her later." She had the most expressive eyes that would betray every thought in her head.

They got big with confusion when she asked me of my whereabouts. They squinted in jealousy when she spoke of my supposed girlfriend. Annie was a girl who laid it all on the table and, back then, I did, too.

"I've been watching All My Children. I keep forgetting we have lab on Wednesday. I'm sorry." I wasn't a show stopper in those days because I hadn't filled out yet. But I had a cute little Huxtable charm going on. I had been with a woman five times, since I lost my virginity at sixteen, and three of those times was with the same woman.

Annie's brows arched over her eyes.

"*All My Children*? Oh my God. Did Jeremy rescue Erica off the ledge yet?"

"No. He chose Natalie instead."

"He did *what*?"

"Well, she's pregnant."

"She's *what*?" And that's how Annie and I started talking about something else besides dissecting frogs. Annie couldn't watch *All My Children* anymore because her VCR was broken and her roommate taped *Days of Our Lives,* which came on around the same time. TiVo was as far away as the flying car so I got her up to speed, which she appreciated, and she impressed me with her knowledge of the show, which I appreciated. "You think Billy Clyde Tuggle is really dead?"

"Oooh, Billy Clyde. You taking me back."

"Well, if Tad survived the fall off the bridge then Billy Clyde should have, too." She snapped her fingers in recollection. "Wasn't that whole Ted Orsini thing stupid? How can everybody in Pine Valley have a twin?"

"I know. It's like the twin capital of the world." She laughed at my joke and we walked to the cafeteria together. I noticed that more women who normally wouldn't give me the time of day, spoke to me, when they saw me with Annie.

"I can't believe they killed Jesse," she said. "I cried like a real person died. My father made me talk to the school counselor."

"Really?" I laughed at her.

"It was so embarrassing." I kept laughing and she punched me in the arm.

"You want to get something to eat?" I said.

"Well, we're standing in front of a cafeteria, aren't we?" I pinched her arm and she threatened to kick me in the knee. I had always found women easier to talk to than men. Always. I was that guy in high school who couldn't get laid because most of the girls saw me as their brother. Good Lord, they'd tell me everything. How they hated their stepfather, about their mother's lump, what boys they had sex with and how big they were, which girls they hated, the intimate details of band practice, the teachers they had a crush on, which teachers they thought they could sleep with, who they thought was a fag, their brother's operation, what they wanted for Christmas, when they had their last period—they'd do everything except gimme some. But I enjoyed talking to them and I'd be lying if I said I didn't.

I had my male buddies but the girls were the ones I'd stay on the phone with for hours and hours. The girls were the ones I shared an emotional bond with. "You're so easy to talk to," Annie said. We got our trays and pushed our way through the crowd. We found a table near the window with a view of the field where a bunch of Q-Dogs where playing touch football. I remember to this day that they all had their shirts off. I couldn't tell you what Annie was wearing but I can clearly remember they all had their shirts off.

"What are you looking at?" Annie said. She followed my gaze to the half-naked frat boys.

"That guy owes me money," I said. That was almost the truth. I had lent Rayford twenty dollars last week. We lived in the same dorm and he had knocked on my door. I knew him from speech class. He had the stocky, powerful body of a collegiate wrestler. When he tapped on my door, he wore only a towel, and was still wet from the shower down the hall. My hands shook when I gave him the money.

"Since you're giving out money, you can throw some this way," Annie said. I chuckled at her. "Who's laughing?" Annie and I began eating together and talking about *All My Children* for that entire first week. We both decided that she would keep tabs on me to make sure I missed no more labs. In turn, I would tape episodes of the show with the VCR I had received as a graduation gift. "Oh, but my stupid roommate won't let me touch her precious VCR. I won't be able to watch the tape."

"You can watch it at my place." I was shocked to hear the words come out of my mouth and I could tell from her expression that she was, too.

But she said, "Well, ok." I never knew if she said that to be polite or not but we exchanged numbers and, the next thing I knew, I had a regular date with Annie every evening for homework, gossip, and soap opera.

We became very comfortable with each other rather quickly. Sometimes, she'd let her leg flop over mine as we sat on the floor in front of the small set tucked right next to the miniature fridge. I had a room to myself because my assigned roommate never showed up but I always had plenty of company. People loved to drop by my room asking for things because I had a fridge and my mother always sent me a care package. I often wondered how these people were raised or if they had parents who cared. They never seemed to have anything at all. I finally learned to say no to the constant requests, but people kept coming anyway, and my room became a hangout area. Rayford stopped by frequently too, usually wearing shorts from wrestling practice and sitting wide-legged on my bed. People got accustomed to seeing Annie there sitting close by me on the floor. We had become a couple before I even asked her.

It's just what folks expected of us.

One day, the fellas were gathered in my room and we were shooting the breeze before Annie dropped by.

"You telling me you ain't hit that yet?" Rayford said. He frowned at me. "You ain't no faggot, is you?" They all laughed. There was Rayford; flopped stomach-down on my bed, sweaty from wrestling as usual. His scent always remained long after he left. There was Peahead, who called himself a preacher but he was chasing tail just like everybody else. He was good singer, too. There was Johnny, a tall southern guy who everybody liked and he would often use the word "melodious" in a sentence. The group clown. And then there was James. James had a large head and, at first, I thought there was something wrong with him but that was just the way his skull was shaped. Red fella. Sweet guy. Dumber than Chrissy Snow.

"Hell naw, I ain't no faggot!" I said.

"Bitch, don't get mad. Here. Come suck my dick and let's be friends." They all laughed again.

"Fuck you, Rayford! Get out!" I was always throwing people out of my room and people would never leave.

"Easy, greasy," Johnny said. "Let's keep everything on a melodious keel."

"Aw, nigga, here you go," said James.

"Must everything be melodious?" I said.

"Aw, shut up, sissy, 'fore I tap that melodious ass." They all threw their heads back in hysterics. I had to do something.

"Don't throw your big head back like that, James," I said. "The weight could snap your neck." The fellas booed my lame attempt at a comeback.

"That's weak," James said.

Peahead the preacher cleared his throat. "Now, now, fellas. Lay off my brother man."

"Thank you."

"If he wants to remain virginal for his wedding night—" They all laughed.

"I'm not a virgin!"

"—then God will bless him abundantly."

Rayford recovered from a laughing and coughing fit long enough to speak. "Look here, bruh. If you don't do something 'bout Annie, then, I just might hit her myself."

"Why? What'd she ever do to you?" James said. We all stared at him.

Johnny broke the silence. "Uh, anyway, Rayford you can't ascond with another man's spoils. That just ain't melodious."

"Nigga, please."

"I mean it. You'd get killed for just joking 'bout another man's woman where I come from."

"So what?" Peahead said. "Where you come from they think PMS mean Saturday night."

"Peahead, I know your melodious ass ain't trying to crack on somebody. Calling yourself a preacher just to get a girl to speak to your ugly ass. How the hell you gonna be a preacher if you ain't got no church?"

"Ain't got no?" I said. "Can we all at least pretend we go to college?"

"I don't need no church," Peahead said. "Moses led the children of Israel for forty years in the desert without a church."

"Yeah." James said. "And it's gonna be at least that long before Annie take off them panties." He elbowed me while they all screeched at me and pointed. I felt like I had a very shiny nose. Something had to be done.

"Yall don't know what you're talking about," I said. "And it's really none of your business, but if you must know, I'm going make Annie a woman tonight."

"Yeah, ok, sissy."

"Praise Jesus."

"You's a melodious lie."

"No, I'm not. I don't expect you to understand this, Rayford, but some men are hung." They laughed at Rayford. "Every time I try to put it in Annie she starts complaining so I let her suck it instead. That way we're both happy."

"Bullshit," said Rayford.

"For real. But tonight she's gonna use some special lube—"

"Lube? You sound like a white boy."

"—some special lube and I promised to take it slow."

"Bitch, please. You ain't packing," Rayford said.

"Let's find out," I said.

"See? I knew you was a faggot."

"Nigga, my dick too big to be a faggot."

"Prove it."

I unzipped my pants and pulled it out. I let it get hard and grow to full size.

"That ain't bad," said Rayford. "But check this out." He pulled it from under the leg of his shorts and let it flop on my sheets. He stroked it a few times and it immediately got hard. He was bigger, by a bit, but I was thicker.

"Check out these melodious jewels," said Johnny in his mad scientist voice. Johnny had a long, skinny, uncircumcised penis that bent to the side when it got hard. "I use that crook to scratch my bitches backs for 'em. As a courtesy." He had nuts bigger than both me and Rayford put together.

"Lord, it's Sodom and Gomorra up in here," Peahead said. "I'll pass."

"Why? You need to pray for a bigger dick?" Rayford said. We laughed at Peahead and I turned to James.

"Your turn, James."

"Naw, I don't wanna play. All yall faggots, you ask me."

"Let's see who can bust a nut first," said Johnny.

"Won't that hurt?" James said.

"He means ejaculate, James," I said.

"Oh I'm Baptist." None of us knew what the hell that meant.

"Go!" I said. We began masturbating rapidly and giggling.

"Forgive 'em, Lord. They know not what they do."

"Shit, gimme some grease or something," Rayford said. I reached behind me and got my Back Alive moisturizer that I used to maintain my Blair Underwood hair. I squirted some in the palm of my hand and tossed the bottle to Johnny.

"Hey, wait up, brother. You got a *head* start." Johnny got his share and threw the bottle to Rayford. He leaned back on my bed against the concrete wall. He spread the gel on his meat from top to bottom and went to town.

"Ok," said Peahead. "Since you heathens are determined to do this, I guess you'll need a guide through your perilous journey." He looked at his watch. "Ok...the second hand is coming to the twelve... and.... go!"

The smacking of lubricated flesh and bouncing fists echoed through the room. "Johnny, can you lend me twenty dollars?" James said. Johnny looked at him like he was crazy and returned his attention to the matter at hand.

"I'm getting close!" I said.

"You a damn lie," said Rayford.

"I'm rounding third," Johnny said.

"Fifty-four seconds," Peahead said.

I really was close but I needed something to push me over the edge. I thought of Annie's big video breast. I thought of stroking them as I had seen in porno films. I thought of dominating and making her mine. I was in a world of my own. "Take this dick, Annie! Take it, bitch!"

"Oooh, Annie! Share your melodious twat!"

"Keep away from her! She's mine!"

"Gimme that fat pussy, Annie!" Rayford said.

"Hey! Knock it off!"

"Ninety seconds!"

We all beat our meat like fiends, watching each other closely for the winning shot, screaming "Annie! Annie!" to the top our idiotic lungs.

And at that moment Annie opened the door. She screamed. I came.

"We have a winner!" Peahead said.

I quivered there, stupefied, weak in the knees, drooling from both heads. Annie screamed like she saw a man being slaughtered. I reached out to her, still coming like a geyser, to comfort her, to explain, to stop her from screaming. Then Rayford popped his load with a holler and Johnny brought up the rear. Semen streamed through the air like confetti while Peahead and James laughed like escaped loons. I could hear doors opening down the hall and concerned voices rumbling in confusion. And Annie screamed and screamed and screamed.

"Shut up and get in here!" I managed to say. "And shut the goddamn door!" She ran at top speed of course. I waddled to the door with my pants around my ankles and slammed it shut.

"Aaahh," said Johnny, his crooked dick still leaking. "Melodious."

"Get out of here! All of you! And I mean it this time!" I snatched the covers away from Rayford that he was using to wipe himself off. "Get the fuck out!" Peahead and James went out leaning on each other in laughter. Johnny said something about going to the cafeteria and Rayford smiled at me on his way out.

"I'll check on you later," he said. I didn't respond. "Don't worry about, man. She gonna be all right."

I leaned my head against the wall. "What am I going to say to her?"

"You'll figure something out. You always been smart. I'll holler at you."

"Ok." He left and I looked at the drops on the floor trying to remember how it all came to this. I called Annie by the time I thought she was home.

"Hello?" Her voice was tense.

"Annie, it's me." She hung up. I didn't know what to do. I plopped on my bed and now wished I had a roommate. I had thought about asking Rayford but I didn't want to look gay.

Why did I have to be this way? Yeah, I was raised by a single mother but so were my other friends and they didn't seem gay. I didn't dare go to the library and check out a book about it. What would the librarian think?

My room was empty and I wasn't used to that. I was an extremely social being for somebody who spent so much time hiding. Normally, Annie would be here watching the soap and my friends would be trailing in and out. But not now.

I was lonely.

I curled up on the bed in the fetal position and tried to figure a way out of this. Rayford was right. I really was smart and if I just sat here long enough then something would present itself to me. It didn't happen. I pulled the covers over my head and caught a whiff of Rayford's scent. I brought the covers to my nose with both hands and inhaled. His hard penis flashed in my mind. I tried to picture it more clearly. It was important to me, vital, to remember every detail of his body. Of how he held it, of what it looked like when he came. I removed the covers from my nose and searched with my hands for his wet spot. I found it.

Then I exhaled.

I touched his seed with my finger and dabbed it on my tongue. The taste inflamed me and I got hard all over again. I searched for more of it, like water in the desert, collecting the precious resource in my hand. I smeared it all over my dick and masturbated again, slowly this time, without racing. Just me and all the time in the world to think of Rayford sitting wide-legged on my bed. Rayford calling me a faggot. Rayford wet from the shower. Rayford's bulge in his wrestling tights. My stomach grew hot and I rubbed more of his manhood on me and stroked with both hands. I heard myself moan before I saw the door open.

Rayford stood there in shock. I either could not or would not stop.

"What you doing?" He said. It was a stupid question. It was stupid of me not to lock the door but it was habit to leave it open. It was instinct that made me keep going. Rayford watched me with narrow eyes. He looked at the covers crumbled around me. "You tripping for real. You know that?" I just kept jacking off slowly. I raised my hips off the bed and thrust in the air like I was making love. I didn't know why but I was giving him a show. I knew it was wrong and I did it anyway. I either could not or would not stop. Rayford locked the door. He took off his shorts and sprang to full attention. I grabbed him and put it in my mouth.

I had never done that before but it felt so natural. He grabbed the back of my head and pushed deeper inside my throat. I tried to move away but he wouldn't allow it. I howled like a woman when I climaxed on his chest. "Aw shuck now," he said. He came in my mouth and I swallowed it all. None of the public health warnings meant a damn to me then. My head spun like I was falling and I twisted my mouth around it to squeeze out every last drop. He withdrew and pulled his shorts back up. I reached out to him to get him into bed. I needed to hold him, to feel his skin on mine. "I knew you was a faggot." Then he walked out the door.

I lay there stunned and mortified still dripping in my filth. What did I do wrong? Why did he participate if he didn't want it? Would he tell on me? Wouldn't he incriminate himself if he did? Man, I was so young. And so trusting. I didn't understand the down low games that men played with each other. It's not good to be that naive. It's just not healthy. Too much can happen to you. People are always expounding the virtues of an open heart but a wide open heart is an easy target.

I wiped myself off and called Annie again. "Hello?"

"Annie, please don't hang up."

"Then don't call back."

"Annie, you don't understand."

"Yes, I do. I thought there was something about you. Not most guys are into soaps."

"Annie, I'm not gay. None of us are! Didn't you hear us chanting your name?"

"That suppose to make me feel better? I don't know what you boys do to get off when you're together and I don't want to know."

"Annie, please. You're being ridiculous. You really think Rayford and those guys are gay?"

"You sure do talk about Rayford a lot."

"We were just playing a stupid game and we shouldn't have done it. I'm sorry. But it looked bad because you came in at the wrong time."

"I'm sure I did."

"Look, why don't you just come on over and I'll explain. We can still watch the tape."

"No thank you."

"But Silver is framing Erica for the murder of Kent Bogart!" She hung up. I finished cleaning myself and got dressed. If I could see her in person then I could explain. I was good at talking people into things. I always had been. I could make everything right if I could just see her.

I climbed down the fire escape on the side of the dorm. I jumped off the landing and into the grass with a roll. I dashed across the street toward the girls dorm at the far end of the quad. I was out of breath, even though I hadn't run that far, and leaned against the brick column in front of the cafeteria. I panted there while people passed by me to get something to eat. I didn't realize how late it was. A smell that resembled some form of meat wafted out of the swinging doors. I reasoned that a well-fed, rested version of me would make a better impression on Annie. So I went inside.

I saw Johnny, Peahead, James, and Rayford near the front of the line. I walked towards them to cut in line like I always did. James saw me first. I waved at him but he didn't wave back. He elbowed Peahead and said something. They all stared at me. Rayford whispered something and they laughed. This laughter was different than the teasing from before. This was the laughter of strangers. Johnny surprised me the most of all. He looked at me like he hated me. Mr. Melodious himself. I got a dreadful feeling in my gut and backed out the door. I bumped into a few Alphas I knew and they said they'd be stopping by later. I nodded and looked back at my friends before I left the building. Rayford glared at me with a smile.

I walked out of the cafeteria and noticed the sky. The sun glowed orange and rested low on the horizon. I looked at the red-brick buildings on the quiet, country campus in this hick college town. I knew this would be the last time I saw it all so I took my time. I stuck my hands in my pockets and strolled back to my dorm admiring the crisp, green landscaping. I nodded at passing students who spoke to me with smiles and fond familiarity. I soaked in my last remaining moments as a popular man on campus. I had a pleasant conversation about nothing with a group of girls from my Lit. class. They sang at the local church and told me Peahead would be preaching his first sermon this Sunday. They asked me if I was coming and I told them I would.

I strolled up the front stairs to my dorm and stopped in the lobby. The gang was watching *The Cosby Show*. I leaned on the back of the sofa to laugh with them at Rudy lip-synching to a blues song like a grown woman. Somebody asked me how Annie was doing and I told them she was doing fine. I studied them hard. I didn't want to lose a single sight or sound. I drew them all in my mind like a careful artist noting things about them I'd never seen before. Like how Betty had a slight lisp and Orson would be kind-of fine if he fixed his teeth. I never realized how much I liked college and I was going to miss it when I left.

I went to my room and packed. I didn't know where I was going or what I would tell my mother. All I knew for sure was that I was leaving. My mother would never pay for another school after I dropped out of this one so I figured I would have to get some type of job. I had always been good at talking people into things. And all while I packed, I kept trying to figure out how Rayford came out of this smelling like a rose.

What did he tell them? Why didn't I confront him? Confront any of them at all? But the way I ran away like that... now I looked like a guilty man.

I dumped old papers in the trash, like my composition on the life of William Blake that earned me an "A," and birthday cards from home, and a poem I had written for the Black History Month committee, and stuff like that. I cleaned the place impeccably. I wanted to make it seem like no one had ever been in my room. I came across a picture of the five of us taken for the campus newspaper. We were goofing around and hanging off the statue of the school's founder. I had gone to the trouble to have it framed. I threw it in the garbage on my way out the door.

True, I could have transferred to another college but I was done with that part of my life. I had been perfectly happy where I was and didn't want to cheapen the experience by trying to re-create it someplace else. There was also the fear that I would fail in such an attempt. Something inside me died when my friends rejected me that day. It was brought back to life by Jesse Chuma and then it died again. My mother didn't understand my sudden departure and refused to take me back in. I didn't blame her. She had done her job raising me and I was grown, after all. One night, I worked up the courage to call Annie again. I waited until late at night when I knew she would be in.

I slammed down the receiver when Rayford answered the phone.

Monster's Mall

"**O**k, Tammy. Let's try this again."

"But I'm tired."

Her fat ass was always tired. "Are you too tired to own a new car?"

"Can't we just take a break?"

"No we can't, Tammy. Because if we take a break now then I won't be able to cold call later. And if I can't cold call later then I won't make my quota for today. Does that make sense?"

"Oooh, the devil is messing with you today, child. You all right?" No, I'm not all right because I'm saddled with you instead of Gary. "Just remember," she said. "No weapon formed against you can prosper." Bitch, if I had a weapon your surplus ass would be feeding a third-world country right now.

"I need you to concentrate, Tammy."

"I need you to concentrate, too. Get all these demons out of here." This woman loves to talk about demons. Like there's room for a demon in there. I think she actually wants to be possessed so she'll finally have something interesting to say.

"Tammy... look... let's just take it from the top."

"That's what I'm trying to do."

"Ok, fine."

"Fine, then." She picked up the copy from her cluttered desk and began.

"The phone, Tammy, don't forget the phone."

"But I ain't talking to nobody."

"I know that." I felt a great strain remaining calm as if trying to bend a spoon with my mind. "But if you talk on the phone now... it won't be such an adjustment to use the phone later."

"I don't think I'd have much adjusting to do."

"Just trust me."

"Trust in the Lord. Lean not onto thine own understanding." I hate this bitch. I looked at her in silence because usually when you do that the other person will start talking. It worked. She picked up the phone with her chubby paw, held the copy in front of her face, and read like a third grader. "Hello? My I speak to John Doe, please?"

"Don't say that."

"But it say so right here."

"But I told you not to say that the last time. Remember? You gotta remember when we go over something or there's no point in going over it."

"I'm sorry."

"If you start off that way then they can tell you're a telemarketer or a bill collector."

"Ok."

"Use the script as a guide. Not a Bible."

"I'll try."

"Ok." I made a damn good living as a telemarketer in a world of Do Not Call lists. If this hallelujah heifer would just listen then she might be able to afford something besides tithes and bad shoes. A busy signal came through the receiver.

"Ooops."

"Goddamn it. Tammy, didn't I tell you to unplug the phone?"

"I know you didn't just take the Lord's name in vain up in here."

"Will you focus? Fuck it. McGhee!" McGhee looked up from his desk. He shushed me because he was monitoring Gary's technique on his manager's phone. The manager phones could tap into every other phone in the office. I slashed across my throat with my finger and pointed to Tammy's phone. He punched a button under his desk and the busy signal died.

"That's better," she said.

"Right. Let's take it from the top."

"Hello? My I speak to John Doe, please?"

"I told you not to say that, you retarded motherfucker!"

"Oooh! The devil is busy in here today!" She burst into tears and everybody stared at me like I evicted Joseph and Mary from the inn. McGhee slapped his hand against his forehead.

"That will be all, Tammy," I said. She ran to the restroom, wailing like a mammy, and I went back to my cubicle to slump in my chair. McGhee appeared over my wall with his Bozo poofs waving at me from above.

"Maybe you should take an early lunch."

"I'm not hungry, McGhee."

"It's not a request."

"Look, I have calls to make."

"I'm sure a super stud like yourself can absorb the loss for one day. Tammy's upset and I don't want you around to aggravate the situation."

"The only thing that could aggravate that woman is a closed buffet. She'll be fine." He just looked at me awhile using my silence trick against me. "This is ridiculous." I snatched my Ralph Lauren blue blazer off the back of my chair and headed out. "You're running a goddamn nursery in here."

I went through the first security door and the secretary was on the phone. I was just about to go through the second security door when she hung up.

"Taking an early lunch, ha?" Great. Now I gotta talk to this fool.

"Yeah." I let the heavy glass door close and seal off my escape. I turned to face her and made myself smile. "How's it going? Hadn't talked to you in a while."

"I knoooww! It's been ages, ha?"

"Yeah."

"Always in such a rush. I usually call Charles for a little gossip but McGhee's always eavesdropping and makes me hang up."

"Well, you know how McGhee is. Tick, tick, tick."

"Oh, I know. Horrible man, ha? My kids say he looks like Bozo."

"I hadn't noticed."

"Yeah. Did I show you the latest picture of my kids?"

"Nuh-uh."

"Well, come on over here."

Doctor Bombay? Calling Doctor Bombay. "All right." I approached her desk and she pried this thick envelope of pictures out of her purse and put her half-bifocals on.

"Now, let's see. This is Reginald at the school play. He's playing Peter Pan."

"Oh, that's nice. You make that costume yourself?"

"I did! Does it show?"

"Not at all."

"Now, this is my oldest, Doris, at the Applewaite boy's bar mitzvah. She's getting taller and taller every day."

"Man, she's something to look at."

"Oh, thank you. She takes after her father. I was never that good looking."

"I don't believe that."

"No it's true. And this is mama's little man at the nursery. He's teething here so this isn't a very good picture. I love that fluffy sweater on him but his father says it makes him look like a fag. What do you think?"

"......................"

"I said what do you think?"

"Oh, he's a cute little boy."

"But do you think that sweater makes him look like a fag? Ha?"

"......................"

The phone rang and she answered. It was her husband by the sounds of it. I walked to the door and she waved at me to wait. I pointed at my watch and shrugged as I pushed my way outside.

A cool breeze hit my face when I stepped onto the sidewalk. I felt wobbly so I moved to the bus stop and sat down. A bus pulled up and people got on. This sissy was smiling at me from his window seat and when the bus pulled away, I shouted, "What the fuck you looking at, faggot?" The guy stood up on the bus and yelled back at me. The passengers jerked around to look and the woman sitting next to him quickly moved away. The bus turned the corner and the people on the bench stared at me. Somebody tapped me on the shoulder.

"You all right?" It was a cop.

"Yes, officer, I'm fine."

"What's going on then?"

"Nothing's going on." I used that same tone with him I always used with McGhee and immediately realized I had made a mistake.

"Can I see some identification, please?"

I took a deep breath. "Look. Officer. Some faggot was giving me the eye and I overreacted. But you know how it is. Or maybe you don't. I'm sure you don't. But these homos are taking over the world. I mean, a man can't even catch a bus these days."

The officer laughed and slapped me on the back. "Just keep your cool next time." He walked away.

"I will. Thanks, officer." I didn't move. My car was right around the corner but I didn't move. I just needed to sit down for a minute. My stomach hurt and I felt like I needed to vomit. But it passed. A woman smiled at me. I got up and walked away.

I looked at the various window displays in the shops as I walked by. I saw this club shirt and wondered if I was too old to pull that look off. I looked in another place that sold vintage T-shirts of beer companies and fast food chains; McDonalds, Pizza Hut, places like that. It made me hungry. I took out my cell phone and hit a stored number.

"Hey, you! Twice in two days. I'm a lucky girl."

"Yeah. You wanna meet at the mall for lunch?"

"Ok! I'll be there in a few minutes. Where are you going to be?"

"I don't know what I'm in a mood for. Just call me when you get there and I'll guide you to where I am."

"I've kinda got a taste for—" I hung up on her. And why not? I was through speaking. She'll be all right. She always is. Kim was the kind of gal who let you take a dump on her so that's exactly what I did. People are like animals. All people. They can be trained. Trained through repetitive example, monitored with reward and punishment, and then seasoned by time. Some behaviors are trained better than others. For example, one can train the homo not to look at a man but the homo will still want to have the man. A dog trained to act like a cat is still a dog inside. Another behavior that can be trained is how one treats a woman. Almost everything from lying to her, to cheating on her, to hitting her is trained behavior that the woman taught the man in the first place. Black women hate to hear that because they're so used to blaming faggots and white women for all their problems. But the bottom line is this: There are some bitches a nigga wouldn't even dream of hitting. In addition, there are plenty of ladies a man would think twice about cheating on. I'm not saying he wouldn't do it but he'd plan that extracurricular activity like the invasion of Iraq. Kim taught me that she's the kind of girl with a high threshold for bullshit. And once I found that out, I never forgot it.

I pulled into the Baldwin Hills Mall parking deck near the Magic Johnson Theater. I might take Kim to the movies if she doesn't get on my nerves too much. I tried to take Tyrone to the movies one time but we don't have the same tastes. Tyrone's the type of fella who thinks Tyler Perry is William Shakespeare so it's best to simply sleep with Tyrone. I walked to the main entrance trying to figure out if I could quit my job. Maybe I could be a manger myself some place else. Who knows? I knew I could manage a sales force better than McGhee, that's for sure. If I showed my résumé and gross sales to the competition then they'd snap me up in no time.

Why didn't I think of this before? A new job would get me away from that stupid secretary and that hapless group of misfits who I've been carrying all this time. But wait a minute. There would just be another secretary and another group of idiots at the new place I go to. What if I started up my own business with my own sales crew? I'm the ultimate salesman. I could sell Big Macs to a room full of cows. Why am I putting up with this trash when I don't have to?

My musings were interrupted by the sight of yet another sissy who was walking in front of me. He wore these snug white wind breakers that his thick butt could barely be contained by. Look at that. I could bury a body in that ass. I normally don't go for this type of guy because he's too much of a punk and you can't take him anywhere. Guilty by association. Although I couldn't take my eyes off him and my dick woke up to check its messages. Look a there, look a there. You can tell how soft it is by the way it bounces. Then, he looked back at me real fast, kinda caught me off guard. I tried to act like I was looking at something else, but he had me, and I heard him go, "Mmm-hmm," or something like that. I stopped to pretend like I had to tie my shoe and let him walk on into the mall. I needed some distance between us in case Kim beat me here. I needed time for my erection to go down as well.

Truth be told, I kinda admire the sissies of the world. Really. I couldn't be out there like that myself but sometimes I wish I could. The sissy is to the gay man what the nigger is to the black man. You don't want an outsider to mistake one for the other. Every time a straight person sees one of those preening, tawdry, bitch-ass queens then they think we're all like that. The secretary feared her baby in the fluffy sweater would turn out like the sissy in front of me.

I, on the other hand, looked like a man. Tyrone, for example, looks and acts like a man. These sissies, however, are cartoons of women, an exaggeration of the feminine. No female I've ever known—not Annie, not Kim, nor any woman I've ever slept with—acts like these sissies do. And really, it's embarrassing. Why don't they just go ahead and get the operation if they're gonna twist around like that? And why do these punks always stare at you like they're trying to hypnotize you or something? Still, it's sometimes suffocating in the closet and the sissies have room to breathe because they don't care what people think. They're brave if you think about it but I don't think about it much.

"His father says that sweater makes him look like a fag. What do you think?"

"I think his father sounds as stupid as the woman who bought the sweater."

That's what the sissy would have said. That's what I should have said. Yeah.

My erection deflated and I walked into the mall and bam! There he was by the post office looking in the window. Who the hell window shops at the post office? He's obviously waiting for me so I act like I don't see him. But I can feel him looking at me and I just keep on walking to the food court.

"Hey you!" Damn it, she scared me and she's so very loud. She threw her arms around me and I hugged her back to show the sissy I was eating fish today. He stared at me and wouldn't look away. Why do they always do that? He thinks he knows me, this faggot, he thinks he has my number. I take Kim by the shoulders and pull her off of me so I can look into her eyes. Then I kissed her. I kissed her long and deep to show him who knew who.

This hootchy mama passing by said to us, "Go 'head on, now. Yall better work." And that was fine because now we were calling attention to ourselves. Now he could see I was off the menu. Kim was lightheaded when we came up for air.

"Let's go back to my place," she said.

"I can't. I have to get back to work." That was almost the truth.

"Oh, what am I going to do with you?" She hugged me again pressing her body against my soft penis. I looked over her shoulder and was disgusted to see the sissy still staring at me with an unimpressed look on his face. He made me hard. "Mmm. Sure you don't want to go back to my place?"

"Knock it off," I said. She laughed at me. I adjusted myself and yanked her by the arm to the food court where we stopped by the pizza place. She insisted on paying for my combo even though I tried to talk her out of it. She was in the mood for the sushi place a few feet down so she asked me to find us a table.

The warm daylight pouring through the glass roof made everything cozy even though we were in the middle of a mall. The noise of toddlers with parents, and cashiers taking orders, mixed with the hiss of fryers. Everything blended into a comfortable background buzz that was soothing to people who were used to hearing noise all the time. The teenagers hadn't invaded the food court yet because school was still in and I was grateful for that. I wasn't used to being here this early and in a way it felt like a mini-vacation. I found a table not too close to the garbage cans but close enough so Kim could still see me. I waved at her to let her know where I was and settled down with my tray, unfolding my napkins, peeling paper off my straw. A generic jazz groove pumped through the speaker system and I took a deep breath. I relaxed for the first time since this hideous day began.

Then I saw him. That sissy again. He made a point to glide in front of me with his helium ass floating on towards the pizza place. He stood right there and looked back at me, then turned around to face the line. I now understood why some gays were bashed. Was he stalking me? Was that it? I did a quick survey to see if Kim had noticed but she was preoccupied with ordering her sushi. What was I so worried about? It's just another sissy in the mall. There's always a sissy in the mall just like there's always a drunk at the bar. It's what they do.

Kim knew I messed around but I led her to believe she had a chance. She still knew, though. She couldn't feign ignorance like those women who take a man softer than they are on a talk show and pretend to be outraged. So what was there to be afraid of? I don't know. I just didn't want this in my life today. All right? I wanted to feel normal for a second. Can I just have a gay break, for crying out loud? I can't stand these damn sissies. Why am I getting so hard?

"Hey you!" Good Lord, does she ever get tired of saying that? "You want a bite?" She picked a spider roll off her plate with her fingers and shoved it in my face.

"No thanks."

"Try it. It's full of protein."

"I know it is, Kim."

"Have some."

"No. See me? Eating pizza? Right now?"

"Can I have some?" I slid her the slice and she bit into it like it was the best thing she ever tasted. "I shoulda got this instead." She talked with her mouth open and closed her eyes, enthralled in her feast. I saw the sissy walking this way. He wouldn't say something to me right in front of her, would he? I know he ain't that bold. Kim was oblivious in the throes of my pizza and somebody could have run up and snatched her purse for all she knew. The sissy came closer and my heart beat so hard I could feel it knock against my sternum. I thought about my mother finding my porn if I died of a heart attack and she had to clean out my condo. I looked at him, and he looked at me, and he came right at me while Kim ate my pizza. Then he turned up his nose and walked right by.

Fucking faggot.

I could hear him settle down behind me. Either directly behind me or off to the side. I couldn't tell and I didn't want to look.

"This is so good," she said. "Can I have it?"

"Just gimme the fucking sushi, Kim!"

"What's wrong with you?"

"Nothing!" I took a breath. "Nothing. If I don't eat when I'm supposed to I get one of those hunger headaches."

"See? Protein. That's what I'm talking about."

I ate the sushi and tried to calm down. "So what's been going on?"

"I painted a landscape yesterday. My first one."

"Really?"

"Yeah, I've been meaning to show my students how but I wanted to make sure I had it down first. Of course no one ever really has it 'down' but I..." *I could hear him moving around behind me. I knew he couldn't be through eating that fast.* "...old professor used to always say count the brush strokes and we all thought he was senile but he swore that if you used at least one hundred brushstrokes in the same direction..." *I don't pretend to be psychic but I could feel him behind me, at least, I thought I could. I put my napkin on my lap to hide my erection and nodded at Kim with perfunctory manners. My pulse thumped quick again.* "...kids think they're just as grown as the teacher is and I'm not making enough money to get killed over these bad children. The principal said just..." *Kim looked over my head in suspicion. My heart was so loud. This is it. I'm about to die with an erection in the middle of the mall and my mother's going to find my porn.*

He slapped me in the middle of my back so hard that it stung me. I spun around in my chair with my fist balled up.

It was Tyrone.

He laughed and patted me on the shoulder. "One day somebody gonna kill your ass. You keep on," Mabel said. Mabel was Tyrone's wife and she looked just like you'd expect a Mabel to look. I'd never met her before but I knew that was her. Tyrone looked kind-of like one of those hunky ex-jocks with a television job but not as smart. He was about fifty or fifty-five years old, something like that, and he still had it. He had impossibly white teeth, a buzzed military haircut, and these little eyes that he always squinted through when he smiled. He talked like he graduated from the Charles Barkley School of Diction. But who cared, really? I was with Tyrone because of what was going on downstairs, not upstairs.

He had a backside that made Taye Diggs look anorexic. He was dark and endowed like he fathered the world. He didn't have washboard abs but his stomach was flat with just enough fat on him to make him look human. His chest was naturally wide, with hefty pecs that he got without serious trips to the gym. Tyrone was just one big corn-fed fucker who knew how to slang some dick. His ass tasted like honey. I swear to God, I could spend a Sunday afternoon just eating his ass.

His wife was a poster child for the woman who had let herself go. She looked sleepy, like she had just rolled out of bed, her hair brushed back off her face. At least she could have worn a hat. She wore a sweatsuit instead. Could you imagine? A sweatsuit to the mall in this day and age? With a fanny pack no less. A fanny pack. What's next? Hunting our own food? And she looked like she had never even heard of makeup. At least Kim always had herself together. Mabel looks like she just gave up. And who knows. Maybe she did.

We made the proper introductions while the sissy behind us pretended not to listen. Mabel went on Kim's side of the table and they talked about what the food court had to offer while I was left with Tyrone.

"What the hell you doing here in the middle of the day? You finally kill your boss?" He laughed with gusto and patted me on the shoulder. I was getting tired of that.

"I decided to take an early lunch," I said under my breath. "And you?"

"Mabel need to get her prescription changed and she couldn't see well enough to drive herself here." I saw the sissy checking out Tyrone. "So, I just took the rest the day off to tend to her. They gots enough orders filled at the plant today anyways so they could spare a man."

"That right? So what's going on?"

"I just told you. What the matter with you? Speak up. You running from the law?" Tyrone laughed at his own dumb joke again but this time he followed my glance to the sissy behind him. He did a quick survey of his wife and Kim and instantly understood. "So you catch that game last night?"

"Yeah, I caught it."

"Oh no you don't," said Mabel. "Yall ain't about to sit up here and talk about no sports. I gotta get my glasses." She rattled on about the particulars of exactly what was wrong with her eyes while the sissy got up and walked to the garbage cans. He dropped his tray, which made a clattering noise, and we all turned around to look at him. He bent over to pick up his tray, giving us a good view of what he had to offer. I quickly turned back to Mabel to listen to her story.

Kim was watching me. I nodded my head at Mabel and took a glimpse at Tyrone. He checked out the sissy, then me, then his wife. Tyrone asked me if I wanted some gum all of the sudden.

"Don't you see me talking, Tyrone?" Mabel said

"Sorry, baby. Want some gum, Kim? Gum?"

"Fool, don't you see these folks eating?"

"That's fine. More for me." Tyrone got his gum from his pocket and put the foil wrapper on my tray.

"Tyrone, have you lost your mind? Did you just put your garbage on that man's plate?"

"It's fine," I said.

"No, it isn't," said Mabel.

"I'm sorry, baby. I wasn't thinking. 'Scuse me. Let me throw this away." He headed to the garbage cans. Tyrone wasn't as dumb as he looked. The sissy was stacking his tray and dumping his plastic plate. I couldn't look at them too long or it would have been obvious.

"...cause my family always had weak corneas and I been nearsighted since I was a child. My mama said...." What was going on over there? How dare that sissy make a move on my man. I mean honestly. This is why I can't stand faggots. Tyrone reappeared, smacking that gum like it was made out of ham, and patted me on my shoulder again. This time, I moved away from his touch. Mabel continued her lecture on the history of eyes, and now, even the friendly Kim seemed bored.

"Woman, you ready to go or not? These folks don't feel like hearing all that."

"I ain't studying you, Tyrone." He laughed and we joined him. "But he right. We gotta go. Nice meeting yall."

"Nice meeting you, too," Kim said.

"Baby, I'll meet you there later. I gotta go to the bathroom." I looked down at the end of the food court and saw the sissy going to the restrooms.

"Ok, then. Don't fall in." She laughed but we didn't. Mabel headed down one end of the mall and Tyrone went to the restrooms.

"Nice people," said Kim.

"Yeah." I realized I hadn't eaten that much.

"Where do you know him from?"

"The bowling alley."

"Oh. Well, is that one of your friends or one of your *friends*?"

"Kim."

"What? I'm just asking."

"Does he look gay?"

"Do you?"

"Look, don't make me regret telling you the truth."

"I'm just wondering if that's one of your down low playmates."

"Down low? What a tired expression. No, Kim. All right? I know him from the bowling alley. He was thinking about joining the league. That's it. Ok?"

"That's good. Good for you."

"Why the hell is that good for me?"

"Because you rarely talk about your other friends. I was beginning to wonder if you had any. And when are we going bowling again? I liked those people."

"Soon. You done?"

"Well, I—"

"I gotta get back to work."

"Oh. Ok." She started to stack our trays.

"Leave it," I said.

"I hate doing that. Somebody has to clean this up."

"That's their job. Come on." I grabbed her by the arm and guided her to the doors.

"Why are you walking so fast?"

"Because I gotta go to the bathroom."

"Why don't you just go to the one in the mall?"

"I hate using those places."

"You are such a snob. Will you go to the bathroom already? You're pulling my arm off." She snatched away from me in a rare act of defiance.

"Pardon me," I said. "But I really gotta go."

"Just use the one here. Quit being a baby."

"If you insist. Thanks for lunch. I'll call you later?"

"Ok." She moved in to kiss me.

"Don't kiss me, baby. I got sushi breath."

"So what? I've got pizza breath."

"Yeah, I know. Bye." I almost ran to the restrooms.

I entered the corridor leading to the restrooms and a mother was holding her son up so he could get a drink from the fountain. I smiled at her and went through the men's room door.

No one was there. Down at the end I saw Tyrone's work boots peeking out from under the stall. He was just standing there, with no telltale tinkle sounds coming from within, but just standing there in silence. No one was with him. I opened the men's room door again and let it slam without exiting. Now I heard rushed whispers. Now I heard Tyrone moan. I tip toed over there and pushed the door open on the stall next to him. I leapt on top of the toilet to get a look.

"What the fuck?" Tyrone said. I looked down at the sissy who was kneeling on the toilet seat so his feet wouldn't show below. I had interrupted his blow job and we exchanged nasty looks. "Man, you...you almost scared me to death," Tyrone said. He acted like somebody walked into the elevator after he just passed gas. I jumped down and ran back to the men's room door. I made sure the coast was clear and pulled the garbage can out of its metal cover through those little swinging doors. I wedged the can under the door knob from inside.

I had done this before. The garbage can would act as both a hindrance and alarm if somebody came to the door. We'd all have plenty of time to go to our separate stalls before the intruder dislodged the trash can and entered. So what if it was mall security? Mall security ain't nothing to be scared of. All they can do is tell us to leave and, in all the times I've done this, it's simply never come to that. I made sure the improvised door stop was secure and hurried back to the stall.

"Get that faggot out in the open," I said. The sissy looked afraid and I loved it. I grabbed him by the back of the neck and pushed his face down between Tyrone's legs; Tyrone let out his predictable groan. Tyrone's always been loud so I put my hand over his mouth. I stuck my tongue between my fingers and into his mouth. I kissed him and pinched his nipples through his clothes. He pulled his shirt up so I could get to them better. I bit them hard because I was still mad at him.

"Easy, baby," he said. I rubbed the rough hair on his chest and watched the sissy's head bobbing on his pride. I became jealous and got on my knees, too. I licked Tyrone's big nuts and slurped them into my mouth. "Oh, yeah. Both yall bitches get some." I moved up on the shaft and took the head away from the sissy the way one dog slips a bone from another. The sissy went back down the shaft then he came back up again and took the head away from me in turn. This time, he went down further than I had. Again, I took the bone from his stubborn mouth with effort, and this time, I went down even further. We competed back and forth in this pole sucking contest while Tyrone went crazy. Now it was my turn.

I took out my dick and tapped the sissy on the forehead with it. "Open up, faggot," I said. "Open your goddamn mouth." Tyrone and I took turns jamming our meat between his sloppy lips. We kept that up for a while and then I was ready for something else.

I popped out of that faggot's mouth and stepped behind him. Tyrone enjoyed having the throat to himself and grabbed both sides of the head. He smiled at me and I back at him. I pulled the sissy's pants down and slapped his round cheeks hard. I knew that had to hurt him so I kept it up. Smacking him, spanking him, making him jiggle. But he never once complained, this fucking faggot. He whimpered, he sighed, he squealed a little, but he never said stop.

I got the lube out of my pocket. I always traveled with lube. Always. Those tiny packs they give you at free clinics or safe sex booths at black expos. It's a perfect little zip-lock pouch that has Astroglide and two rubbers in it. I squirted some on the tip of my finger and jabbed my finger in his clean shaven hole. I rolled on the rubber, grabbed myself by the base, and slid the tip between his crack. Tyrone looked high. He nodded at me with his eyes half closed in ecstasy.

"Wear it out, baby," he told me. I pushed in slow until the sissy yelped then I rammed him up to his guts. He tried to scream but Tyrone held his head down and gagged more meat in his mouth. I restrained the sissy by both his wrists and twisted them behind his back.

And now was the time for lessons to be taught. Lessons about respect. There are rules. He shouldn't have been staring at me when I was with my woman. Faggot, don't you dare approach me unless I tell you to. And never in the presence of my woman. Don't sabotage my game. Don't ruin everything I'm maintaining. Silly little sissies get killed for such transgressions.

And another thing. He shouldn't have come into this bathroom with Tyrone. Tyrone is *my* man. He belongs to me in a way his wife can never comprehend. Their legal ceremony in the eyes of God is hardly my fault or my problem. Tyrone married Mabel because society told him to. But he's mine. I'm the only person he's truly himself with. I'm the one who really knows him. Not the acceptable alpha male version of himself but the real him. The real Tyrone.

He's scared of heights, for example, because his father taught him how to swim by throwing him off a hill into a lake. He almost drowned six times before he got it right. Six. Now, he can swim just fine, but when he takes the kids to Disney World, he watches from below while they enjoy the rides up high. And during that time, Mabel whines that he doesn't get involved enough. He would never share that story with her because he doesn't want to show a weakness but he didn't have a problem telling me. Mabel doesn't get it, for instance, that Tyrone's favorite color is burgundy. Not red. His mother died of liver cancer when he was just a little boy and he put her burgundy scarf in the casket to go with her. His father scolded him but he knew his mother always loved that scarf. One time, Mabel gave him a red tie and said, "I know that's your favorite color." He corrected her by saying he liked burgundy instead and she told him it was the same difference. He was so angry when he told me about it. I had never seen him that way before. Yeah, I know Tyrone better than his wife, his four brothers, and those homely looking children who take after their unfortunate mother.

Tyrone belongs to me the most and this sissy needs to understand that. This punk has been a problem ever since I walked into this mall. I tried to ignore him but he wouldn't let me. So this is what it's like to have my attention. "Happy now?" He struggled and squirmed while we tore him up from both ends. He might have been trying to say stop. I don't know. And who cares? He shouldn't have been messing around in a toilet with two strange men in the first place.

8

Not Today

I've got my eye on Dante again. Every time he comes in the gym he still pretends like he doesn't see me. Like what happened between us last time was just a dream. He's probably straight, and curious, or either gay and fighting it. It happens.

Kim accused me of not having any friends but that's not true. I just don't have a need to surround myself with a gaggle of people to feel secure. One of my acquaintances is a married gay guy named Laurence. His wife knew he was gay and married him anyway. They just have an understanding. Some women don't like being challenged and, quite frankly, are emotionally lazy. If they get hurt then they tend to shut down instead of moving on to the next guy like a normal person would.

Those are the kind of women who will marry a queen in order to feel safe. Even a queen can get it up for a woman on occasion and now they can pat themselves on the back for presenting the in-laws with a grandchild.

Everyone just ignores how effeminent these guys are because at least they're married and there's a child involved. The gay guy is usually heavily involved in a church or local politics or university life. People don't say anything about it because the guy has power. Or they tell themselves he's just artistic. I'm telling you, I see it all the time.

It's not just that straight women ignore the elephant in the room. They ignore the rampaging elephant with diarrhea in the room. Yes, there are real straight men with limp wrists and soft voices who cross their legs in a certain way. But come on.

My friend Laurence, who I see at the club on occasion, married one of these quiet gals who just didn't want to be hurt anymore and fathered her a child. He's invited me to the little girl's birthday parties but I've always turned him down. Laurence is way too much of a queen for me to be seen with around straight folk but I enjoy talking to him on the phone. He's an excellent and accurate source of gay gossip. Laurence used to work in the A&R department of a major record label so he knows all the rappers who are gay, all the divas of soul who mess around, all the sports stars who dip, and all the actors who are married for PR reasons. He always likes to tease me with information by saying something like, "I really shouldn't be saying this, honey, but a certain gangster rapper is putting the bone on the body guard." If I ask him who it is then he'll claim he can't tell me because careers could be ruined and all that jazz. I learned a long time ago that if I just let Laurence talk he'll eventually spill the tea because he can't help himself. He can always spot who's gay and who isn't. It's infallible. It's not even gaydar. It's a homo omniscience. I decided to ask him about Dante.

"He's gay. But, child, you better leave that fool alone."

"Why?" I was clipping my toe nails while talking to him on the phone.

"That boy crazy."

"Crazy how?"

"Does it matter?"

"Answer the question."

"Oh, honey, I can't say. Lives could be ruined. I can only show you the light. I can't help it if you squint."

"Ok. So how's your daughter doing?"

"She's growing like a weed. She placed third in a spelling bee last week."

"That's great."

"Yeah. She could have won first place if we had drilled a little harder."

"What grade is she in again?"

"Fourth."

"Fourth grade, huh?"

"Yeah, child. Just as grown as she wanna be."

"That right?"

"Gonna make me smack her ass."

"Well don't do that."

"I'm just playing. I ain't gonna hit my baby doll. That's her mama's job. But she getting so big. I know the boys are gonna be after her soon and I'm not ready for all that madness."

"What if the girls are after her soon?"

"Come again?"

"Nothing."

"I heard you, bitch. You trying to be funny?"

"They say it's genetic."

"The only thing my baby doll gets from me is a razor sharp wit and her show-stopping beauty."

"Well. As long as she has a skill."

"You a trip."

"That's what they tell me."

"Mmm-hmm. So Mr. Dante, huh?" I don't say anything because I know he wants me to.

"What happened to ole fine-ass Tyrone?"

"Ain't shit happened to him."

"Yall had another fight?"

"No. I saw him in the mall the other day. He's fine."

"Then why you so worried about Ricky Martin?"

"First of all, you racist drag show, Dante's way finer than Ricky Martin and doesn't look a damn thing like him. Secondly, if Tyrone can have a wife then I'm sure I can have a boyfriend."

"Boyfriend? Bitch, you sound like you in the fourth grade yourself."

"Ok. Lover then."

"Too graphic."

"What then?"

"Your partner."

"Partner?"

"Yeah."

"I've always despised that term. Partner. What the fuck are we doing? Opening up a dental office together? What's the matter with lover?"

"It's just so sexual."

"So what?"

"So what happens when yall ain't having sex no more?"

"Then you're married."

"You a mess."

"You gonna tell me or not?"

Laurence told me that Dante messed around all right. He has a baby even though he doesn't live with the mama. He's slept with a couple of guys who Laurence knows from sex clubs. I've always been tempted to join a sex club but I'm just too tense about it. I don't want to have to show my driver's license, and register, and have my name in a computer. Laurence swears that they're discreet. They would have to be to in order to stay in business. But I just have this thing about being on a file. It doesn't matter with Laurence because everybody can tell he's a faggot anyway but I can still pass.

I remember when the AIDS epidemic first hit, a lot of brothers didn't want to go to the clinic because they said once your name gets on that computer then it would go all around the country. Every government institution, every insurance company, every background check for a job and what not, would reveal you had AIDS or HIV. It sounds like sci-fi superstition but a lot of people still believe that whether it makes any sense or not. That's why so many men drive out of town to get treated. That's one of the reasons why so many men don't get tested at all. They'd really rather not know.

So anyway, Dante is definitely all the way gay and—get this—Chuckles is his lover.

"That fat tub of goo is his lover?"

"His partner."

"You're lying. You gotta be."

"Sorry. It's back to black and white, Dorothy. And give back them slippers. Wake up, bitch."

According to Laurence, and I wish he was wrong but I know he isn't, Chuckles, whose real name is Henry of all things, is Dante's live-in lover and they've been together for about three years. I automatically assume that Dante's being kept but no. He's got a good job working for UPS and pays most of the bills. Chuckles, or Henry, has been on disability for some kind of nonsense and gets a crazy check from the City of Los Angeles.

"A crazy check?"

"Yeah, honey."

"I thought you said Dante was the crazy one."

"He is. You ever seen that scar on his arm?"

"Yeah, I've seen it. It's hot."

"It's manslaughter."

"What?"

Laurence said Dante got into a gun fight with some Crips because they were harassing Henry. It happened in Inglewood when Henry used to deliver pizzas for Domino's. He got confused in his delivery truck because he wasn't used to being on that side of town. Apparently, he started getting real nervous. Nobody knew why he tripped out, he just did, and instead of calling Domino's and telling them he couldn't find the address, or driving back to the store, he sat there and proceeded to eat all the pizzas. Every last single one of them.

"You gotta be joking."

"Nay, sweetness. 'Tis true." There had to be at least ten pizzas in the truck. He took them out of the thermal bag, scooped his hand in the center of the hot sizzling cheese, and tossed it into his mouth. Even before finishing one pizza he'd move on to another. He had to have been in there for a while because some of the Crips, who were playing basketball on a nearby court, caught on to what was going on and attacked the truck just for fun. They taunted Henry and several of them rocked the truck back and forth with him trapped inside. During this time, Henry ate and cried while being bounced around the vehicle.

"That's the funniest fucking thing I ever heard." I threw my toenail clipper down hard on the floor and got down on my knees shaking with laughter.

"Satan, you have a call on line 666."

"I can't help it. Oh... oh... Lord. Wait a minute... lemme breathe..." And again I was taken over by the giggles.

"Just let me know when you're through. I have nothing else planned."

"Ok, ok... Heh!... Tell me more. Please." Dante was dropping off a kilo in the area back in the days when he used to do that sort of work and saw the Crips attacking the truck. He pulled out his gun and ran straight to the action firing one warning shot into the air. "Why did he get involved at all? Why not just call the cops? He could have been killed."

"I don't know, honey. He must have just looked at poor Henry and saw a homo in distress."

"But how would he even know he was gay? Did they know each other from before?"

"Nope. He just saw him and fell in love."

"With him? You're crazy. He had to feel sorry for a fat boy in trouble, that's all."

"Are you a size-ist?"

"A what?"

"A size-ist. You called me a racist. Do you have a thing against big people?"

"I think you just made up a word."

"You always got something to say about fat people. Did some fat boy take your Scooby-Doo lunch box in junior high? Tell mama your pain."

"How could a fine specimen like Dante could fall for somebody like that? And to put his life on the line, too?"

"Oh, yeah, child. Ran in there telling them to get away from that boy. And they started just a shooting and the next thing you know Dante done killed one of them Crips."

"What?"

"Uh-huh. Dante always packing, child. That fool sleep with a gun. Brush his teeth with a gun. But the cops cut him a deal when he snitched on his drug supplier and murder was reduced to manslaughter. He did a little time and knocked up his old girlfriend during a conjugal visit. And ole Henry waited for him 'til he got out. Visited him every week while he was in there, too."

"I don't believe this. How did Henry end up getting a crazy check from the city?"

"Child, he worked for the sanitation department and there was some kinda incident with a dead dog and super glue that I'm still a little fuzzy on. Long story short is Henry gets paid to be nervous."

"Unbelievable."

"Which part?"

"All of it." I threw some shorts in my gym bag and we didn't say anything for a while. "Well, obviously they have an open relationship. Chuckles was looking right at our little dry hump in Bally's that I told you about."

"Maybe. But aren't you tired of sharing a man? Why move from sharing Tyrone to sharing Dante?" I didn't respond. "Sometimes one man looks at another and sees something that he can't do without. Don't worry about it, baby. It'll happen to you one day."

"Laurence, please. You're a fag married to woman. Spare me your Homo-Wan-Kenobi routine."

"I can see you're regressing to your special place right now so I'm gonna go on about my business. But what I have works for me, sweetness. I got my daughter and I'm happy. What you got? Bye." He hung up. Little bitch.

I put some socks in my gym bag and got a frozen bottle of water that was halfway thawed from the fridge. I added that to the bag and left my apartment.

I walked down the hall to the elevators and could hear one of my neighbors vacuuming. Somebody else was cooking spaghetti and my mind flashed forward to figuring out what I wanted for dinner. I'd probably just order something from Pink Dot but that was getting old and I wouldn't mind having a hot cooked meal. Maybe I should take some vacation time and go back home for a while. I hate my hometown but I love my mother, and some of her food would make me feel like a part of the world right now.

I don't know why I'm letting Laurence get to me. I jab the elevator buttons again and again. I stare out the lobby window at the mountains while I wait. Frankly, I know good and well that I don't want a lover. If I wanted that I could have Kim over here right now stuffing a turkey and hanging curtains. I'm not planning on coming out of the closet and I sure don't want to live with a man. That would simply look too funny since I'm way past the age where having a roommate is normal. Besides, I like my privacy. And I like sleeping with whomever with no strings attached.

Laurence is crazy, that's all. I have a job with a salary that plenty of people would kill for. I live in an envied condo and have the freedom to be myself. Well, maybe not myself but the freedom to come and go. And that sissy is bragging about his child? So what?

Is that all he has going for him? I don't want a noisy, needy, phlegm-filled child in the first place. Why don't I just put my cash in a paper shredder instead? He's turning into more of a woman everyday. Up there bragging about a child. Please.

The elevator comes and I get on with this older white man and his Old English sheep dog. He's always giving me the eye and I'm always ignoring him. He probably guesses I'm gay. He's probably seen some guys come to my apartment and figured it out.

"How are you doing?" he said.

"Fine."

"Hot enough for you?" I don't even answer and put on my earphones. Yeah, it's rude but these white sissies really do need a brick wall to fall on them. They have all these Mandingo fantasies and they're pushy and more presumptuous than any stalker could ever be. I once got in a fight at a white club because this Jack McFarland clone just walked up and put his hand on my crotch. White sissies are good for that. I'm not a bigot or anything but I prefer to party with my own and sleep with my own. They at least have to be Latino to make Mr. Dickinson rise.

The elevator opened on the parking level and I thought of Dante again. *Sometimes one man looks at another and sees something that he can't do without.* What gay greeting card did he steal that from? I wasn't in love with Dante. I knew that. But it pissed me off that he would be in love with Henry, of all people. Henry? Why should Henry be able to score a guy like Dante? Fat and crazy too? I don't get it. I get in my car and hit the remote to open the gates.

I carefully check both ways of the tricky exit to the street. There have been several car accidents here because of the blind spots created by hedges and off street parking. I've complained to the management and they've cut back the hedges but it's still a pain in the ass. The one time I was late to work was because somebody had an accident and blocked the exit for an hour while the cops came and investigated. The driver got banged up pretty good, too. I inch out, bit by bit, with some jerk behind me riding my bumper, and sure enough, I almost get hit. I turn around, and shoot the guy behind me a bird, then head straight down Western.

Aren't you tired of sharing a man? I don't believe this. I'm actually letting Laurence get to me. I don't know if I'm tired of sharing a man or not. It's not something I've ever thought about really. If you're in the closet, the only men you meet are those who belong to somebody else. That's just the way it is. They either belong to another woman or to another man. It's not sharing. I'm borrowing the man at best, and hell, I give him back. The only alternative to not sharing a man is to live a straight life or come out of the closet.

But let's get real.

I pull up to the gym and see the usual muscle queens getting out of their leased sports cars and making their way to the entrance. I hear a muffled voice through a megaphone. Is somebody making a speech? It's probably one of those supplement stores hawking creatine powder or a water cooler company giving away free gym bags. Maybe it's one of those people giving away tickets to television shows.

I've been here in LA for eight years and I've only seen one sitcom. The show was funny, at first, but it got kind of dull as the evening went on. The audience had to sit there, through take after take, and none of the actors knew their lines. Initially, it was fun to watch them make bloopers but then that got old, too. How could they be making that much money and not know what they're supposed to say next? Believe me, it's better to watch tv on tv.

I used to fool around with this actor out here. He was beautiful and I liked him just fine. We had problems because he was convinced that he would be a star so he was deeper in the closet than I ever was. It was tedious. He was always afraid our sex was being secretly recorded and thought I was going to sell the tape to the tabloids after he "made it."

Like I don't have anything better to do than wait for him to swim upstream to his one-in-a-billion chance at stardom so I can blackmail him. He was great in bed but I had to let him go. He refused to go into an adult book store on Sunset with me because he thought the footage on the security camera could be sold to *Entertainment Tonight*. He had an audition for a Bruce Willis movie later that week so he was covering all his bases. That was the last straw for me and I stopped returning his calls. Maybe he will be a star one day. I saw him on a soap once, in a bit part, and he was interesting to look at with his clothes on as well.

So he crossed my mind when I walked to the gym from the parking lot listening to the garbled voice shouting through the megaphone. He used to pick up free passes to television shows in front of the gym and that's what I thought all this commotion was about.

The sunlight blinded me when I stepped out of the dark parking deck. I reached for my shades and that's when I saw it. There was a stage set up in this parking lot across the street and down the block from the gym.

A rainbow banner stretched across the stage. There had to be at least two hundred people there. There were black drag queens and people in wheelchairs, with AIDS hospice signs, and their attending nurses. I saw mahogany go-go boys wearing fuchsia he-bitch pants and white tank tops. I saw older black men, with their arms around each other, who looked like they could be the guy next door or the plumber. Black bull dykes were holding hands while their kids played in front of them. They brought kids to this thing? Many hot lesbians, the kind who straight men fantasize about, were also there with their piercings, and their midriffs, and their Goddess attitudes.

Multiple colors popped from one side of the scene to the other. There were bright pink poster board signs that read, "We're L! We're G! We're B! And We're T!" Gold banners flapped on the fence near the entrance with bold red letters saying, "Black Gay Pride Means I Don't Hide."

What the hell? Groups signed in at a registration table covered with a sky blue cloth. The parking lot was full of blacks, browns, reds, and yellows with their cornrows, their afros, their sleek extensions, and bodacious braids. It was an ebony rainbow.

What are they doing here? The Fourth of July gay pride thing on the beach doesn't start for a few more months yet. Who are they? Why are they this close to the gym? And who is that man they're all looking at?

He stood in the middle of the stage with the megaphone. It was the only time in my life when I didn't care if somebody caught me staring at a man. Beauty is too weak of a word to describe him. Beauty has been overused on the overexposed far too often. This man surpassed blunted beauty's need to just be seen. This man was—right. That's all he was and all he needed to be. This man was just right. I instantly doubted I could be right for him but that had nothing to do with my desire to have him.

I blindly accepted a flyer from a guy who was handing them out to people coming from the gym. A woman in front of me crumbled it up and threw it on the ground after she read what it was. The man on the stage was speaking but I couldn't really hear what he was saying. That was a horrible megaphone. I would have to go closer if I wanted to hear. I would have to risk people seeing me and thinking I was one of them.

I crossed the street and wasn't paying attention to where I was going because a car honked at me and then another one. I made it to the other side and proceeded by degrees to the gate while I hid my shaking hands in my pocket. On stage, another fella with dreads and wire-rim glasses took the megaphone from the speaker and gave him a mic. He did a brief "Test, testing," into the mic and the audience applauded their relief. I could hear him much better now.

He said, "...we can't afford to hide any more." I would still have to get closer. I looked back at the gym where I saw Dante and Henry going inside. Dante nodded at me and I ignored him. I either could not or would not stop. "...can't let Bernice King and Ken Hutherson keep telling us that we don't matter enough to be protected nor respected. We need to be as aggressive as these conservative fanatics are. We need to fight back. They're damn right there's a cultural war going on. And we damn well better win it!"

He was so tall on stage that he looked like a giant. I leaned against the chain link fence and put my fingers through the holes. I wasn't ready to go in yet. It was a miracle that I had come this close at all. It was all his fault. He drew me to him and I resented him for it.

"Come on in, brother." It was the guy from the stage with the dreads and the glasses. He looked like he could be an African-American history teacher. I shook my head no and he smiled. "Well, take a flyer then." He gave me the flyer and I compared it to the one I already had.

The first flyer advertised a strip show at The Circus. There was a picture of a popular Latino dancer in his thong and underneath that was a blurb about HIV testing. The second flyer had a picture of the man on stage. He had a brown bald head and direct brown eyes. I had a feeling he knew me but that was impossible. I felt he had known me for a very long time. His eyes implied that lying to him was a waste of time. Underneath his picture was the symbol of some gay organization and his name.

His name was Emmanuel Keys.

Maybe I should go inside. I scanned the perimeter to see who might be looking at me. Nobody was. All eyes were on him.

"Let yourself be seen. You deserve to be seen. There is nothing wrong with you. Don't let people use the Bible as a weapon to attack your right to exist. If your people were not kidnapped from Africa, and forced to worship a new God, under the threat of castration or death, then you don't know what you'd believe in. It's strange that the Kings and the

Dollars of the world conveniently forget that while they damn us with the same religion the masters beat into their ancestors hundreds of years ago." The people clapped and cheered. He raised his hands to quiet them and his big arm flexed without effort. "I believe everybody has to make their own decisions, yes, but I urge all gay people, especially people of color, to go ahead and come on out of the closet. I know it isn't easy. But I've been in and I've been out and being out is better.

"When you're out they have to deal with you because you're already in their schools. When you're out they have to recognize you because you're already in their work place. When you're out they come to know you because you're already in their families. They can't pretend you're just some pedophile on the evening news or a celebrity with an agenda they can't relate to. When you're out you can live a more healthy life because being in the closet puts you under constant physical and emotional strain. Listen to me. I know what I'm talking about.

"When I was in the closet, for example, I made poor choices in men. Because when you're closeted, you are agreeing with the homophobes that there is something wrong with you. And when you think there's something wrong with you... you attract the kind of losers who you think you deserve. When I was in the closet, I lied to my family and was never really present with them. I remember one Christmas when I went home for the holidays and I was devastated because one of these dead-end relationships was over. But I couldn't tell my mother and sister why I was so depressed. So I pretended to have a good time, thus, being only half myself with the people who mattered most to me. Being in the closet caused me to maintain friendships with viciously homophobic straight people that I should have let go of a long time ago. Instead of spending years laughing at their jokes about faggots and AIDS.

"Lastly, being in the closet confined even my gay friendships to people who were just as messed up as I was since that was the best I thought I could do.

"Now, I don't want to act like my life was a tragedy because it wasn't. I have many happy memories and I'm grateful for my life. But as I got older, the closet became more cramped. And I just got plain tired of lying all the time and feeling like there was something fundamentally wrong with me. We've all heard that tired cliché that says we only use ten percent of our brains. Ten percent of our potential. Well, I finally had to ask myself, that if it's true we only use ten percent of our potential… what if my other ninety percent is gay?" The crowd burst into wild applause. I looked back down the street at the gym and didn't see anyone I knew. All I had to do was step inside the gate. The applause receded and he continued. "If I could get in a time machine, I'd go back to my younger self, when I first came here at twenty-four years old and say, Emmanuel, I've got good news and bad news.

"The bad news is: this is not a phase. So this little plan you had to come to Los Angeles, and sow your little gay wild oats, before you got on with your real life, is not going to work." The crowd laughed and he paused for them to die down. Then, I swear to God he looked right at me. I turned around to see if someone was standing behind me but there wasn't. He was looking at me all right. When the crowd got quiet, he said, in a soothing voice, "The good news is that it's ok. You don't have to be anybody other than who you are. There is nothing wrong with you. The people who say you are flawed are incorrect. You have to be strong enough to invalidate the alien opinions of your limited worth."

I felt the world slant while I stayed still. I looked at his face and felt my heart make room. The crowd applauded Emmanuel Keys and he stepped offstage. A woman with a guitar took his place and people rushed to shake his hand. He smiled at them and stole glances at me.

Sometimes one man looks at another and sees something that he can't do without. Don't worry, baby. It'll happen to you one day.

Maybe. But not today. I put the flyers in the trash and walked away.

9

Some Of My Best Friends Are Straight

I lie here in the afterglow of masturbation and keep thinking about Emmanuel Keys. A guy like that probably already has a lover and being with him would require too much of me. I'm not ready to come out of the closet. I'm not ready to fight the whole world. I'm just not. But I'm tired of being alone so there's only one thing left to do.

I've got to make this thing work with Kim.

I give her a call and invite her bowling. Tuesday night is league night and she eagerly accepts as I knew she would. As I get ready for our date, I can't help but wonder what's wrong with a woman who would want a man like me. How come she's not strung out over some other player? Maybe she is, for all I know. I wouldn't expect her to talk about her other men any more than I do. She's an attractive woman and men undoubtedly hit on her all the time. Surely she does something else with her life besides wait on me to call. However, somehow I know that Kim can't move on. Somehow I know she's just as alone as

I am. She's comfortable with me and I won't require much of her. She's the perfect girlfriend for a fag.

We met in front of Jerry's Deli and walked in together to rent our shoes. I couldn't wait to try out my new bowling ball. It was a Hammer Road Hawg with a perfect bridge that I got for a great price online. Anyway, I saw Tank and Jennifer with Lamar and Stacie at the counter getting their shoes. So I said, "We're not giving lessons, kiddies. Only pros tonight."

"Aw, go to hell," said Tank. We called him Tank because he was a large, solid man. He played ball in school until an injury sidelined him and he became a youth counselor. His wife, Jennifer, was a nurse from Phoenix and a wonderful bowler. I always wanted her on my team. Lamar drove a truck and was out of town a lot where he cheated on his wife, Stacie, all the time. Cheated with women, I mean. These were the only straight people I spent time with outside the office and for the most part everything was cool. There was the occasional fag joke but nothing I couldn't laugh off. What the else was I going to do? Tell them they were being homophobic? Oh yeah. That'll go over real good. I pushed thoughts of Emmanuel out of my mind.

"Yall remember Kim, right?"

"Hey, girl," said Stacie. She wore a big T-shirt with a picture of Tu Pac on it, which was a little young for her, and she was ten months pregnant. She never let a little thing like having another baby affect her game. "How you doing?"

"I'm fine, Stacie. How's it going? Hi, everybody."

"Ready to get whooped?" Jennifer said. She got her change back from the cashier and got her size elevens off the counter.

"I got a better idea," Kim said. "Let's switch up this time and play boys against the girls."

"Bad idea," I said.

"No, see, I'm still learning, and from what I can tell, the women are the best bowlers. So why not side with winners?"

"Oh-oh," said Tank. "She leaving you already."

I placed my hand over my heart in mock pain. "Is this a sign of things to come?"

"Not a chance," said Kim. She threw her arms around me and gave me the tongue. I was surprised but kissed her back.

"You don't know what to do with that," Lamar said.

"And you do?" Stacie said. They laughed while we continued to kiss.

"Player, player," said Tank. "Ease up. Get a room." I kissed Kim because I wanted to. Not just to show them I was straight. Kim had put up with my nonsense long enough. The least I could do was to treat her better. I wanted to reward her for being a trouper. I was determined to show her a good time tonight. Tonight, I would be the perfect boyfriend. I mean partner.

We began our game in the far lane by the wall. Tank and Lamar ordered submarine sandwiches and the ladies ordered pizza. I wanted a chef salad.

"A chef salad?" Tank said. "What's the matter? You on a diet?"

"Don't take this the wrong way, Tank, but some folks can't eat the equivalent of a small human."

"Oh, come on," said Kim. "Live a little." She sat in my lap and stuck her pizza into my mouth. "This makes up for the one I stole last time." We smiled.

Stacie grabbed Kim's arm and pulled her off me. "No fraternizing with the enemy. It's your turn. You're up." Kim took her address on the lane and held the ball awkwardly.

"You guys know the rules," she said. She had this thing about being looked at when she bowled. We all turned away and Jennifer giggled. We would know by her groans of despair or happy screams whether she did any good and the computer kept track of our scores.

I patted Stacie's round stomach while Kim bowled in secret. "I think it's pathetic the way you're holding that baby in just to get a little extra attention. I mean, come on. How long you been pregnant again? Two years?"

"Feel that way," said Lamar.

Stacie punched my arm. "It's only been ten months last week. All the women in my family are late."

"That's just what she said when she blew my high that night," said Lamar. "I'm late."

"Hush, fool. These doctors don't be knowing nothing. A baby comes when it wants to."

"When you finally gonna have some kids, brother?" Tank said. "You ain't shooting blanks, are you?"

"I don't know. I never looked." We heard Kim squeal and clap her hands. Stacie leaned down to me and whispered in my ear.

"Try to treat this one right. You hear me?"

"Stacie, stay out that man's business."

"Shut up, fool, and stay out of mine." Stacie peeked at Kim who was taking an inordinate amount of time to be at one with the ball and stare at the pins. She pointed in my face and spoke in low tones. "You remember my girlfriend? The one I set you up with? She ain't stopped talking yet 'bout what a dog you is. The least you could have done is called her after you got into her panties. I see that girl in church sometimes and it's so embarrassing."

"Come on. You don't look that bad." She smacked my arm again.

"Just treat this one right. Ok?" Kim cussed and groaned at a gutter ball.

"I hear you, Oprah, and I obey." She rolled her eyes and I stood to take my address. Kim seemed discouraged. "Shake it off, baby." I gave her a quick smack on the lips. "It's just a game." She smiled and sat down to listen to Jennifer's tips about lifting the ball and keeping her elbow close.

I got my honey from my bag while the fellas "oohed" and "aahed." I looked at the maples in formation. I took four smooth steps, released the ball, and blew the rack. The men cheered while the women booed. My ball returned and I took it in hand. Once more, without much study, I released and followed through. The ball echoed down the oiled lane amidst the clatter of neighboring pins. The intercom blared in the background telling people their order was up. The Road Hawg glided on the scenic route to the head pin. It was a delicate tumbler and down they all went. Set 'em up and knock 'em down. If only life could be this simple.

Kim hugged me and the women reminded her I was playing for the other team. We all had a good laugh about that and I decided I would break down and get some harmful yet yummy carbohydrates after all. To hell with it. I'll spend some extra time on the treadmill tomorrow. Besides, women didn't mind a little fat around the middle. Only men get hung up on stuff like that. Maintaining washboard abs is such hard work that I ought to get paid for it. I'm positive there are way more homos in the world with washboard abs than straight folks. I have no way to prove that but I know I'm right.

After a while, everybody decided they wanted more food as well so I wrote down their orders on the back of a napkin. Stacie tried to give me some money but I said, "It's on me. Save it up to buy your baby a new daddy." Lamar got up to box with me while we all laughed.

"Watch it, nigga," said Lamar. "I know Tony Soprano." I left to get the food and winked at Kim. She was so radiant, so happy. I hadn't seen her like that in… well I hadn't seen her like that. She was looking good, too. I mean really. There are worse fates that could befall a man. I looked forward to munching out and headed to the food counter.

I halted to let some kids run past me to the video games. Kids. The secretary's baby in the fluffy sweater. Laurence's fourth-grade spelling prodigy. Stacie's bulging belly. I'm surrounded by them.

The place is filling up so I'm glad we got here early. Almost every lane is full now and a large group of black folks just came in. Must be a church group or something. I paid for the food and got my receipt. Then, I remembered I hadn't washed my hands. Tank and Lamar always kid me about that and ask me if I want a manicure, too. But fuck 'em. There are some things I won't do to fit in with straight men and eating with dirty hands is one of them. I know my turn to bowl is coming up soon but it'll keep. One of the guys will take my turn or they can spend the time to help Stacie think up less ethnic baby names. The last thing our community needs is yet another Laquondra or Lasheequa.

Anyway, Kim's conversation well never ever runs dry. People like her. They do. She has a quality that makes you want to care. I guess that's why I've stayed with her longer than any other woman I've dealt with. She's put up with a lot from me and I think I'll start giving back. I mean, why not? It's not like she's awful or anything and the sex is good. It's not great but it's good sex for a woman.

I go to the restroom and enjoy an unfamiliar peace while washing my hands. The warm water feels so comforting on my wrists. I squish the white foam between my fingers and hum one verse of *Old McDonald Had a Farm* because that's how long one should wash your hands to kill all the germs. Somebody comes out of the stall and washes their hands next to me. I think I feel them looking at me but that's not even where my head is tonight. This is one of the few times I came to a public restroom to actually use the facilities.

"Don't I know you from somewhere?" Emmanuel Keys said. He looked even better up close. Laurence would describe him as dick-licious. I was stunned and stared at him while the water ran.

"What are you doing here?" I said. I must have sounded angry because he seemed a bit insulted.

"Take a guess," he said. He made a gesture at his bowling shirt that read, in big bold letters: *Black Balls*. Underneath that was, *The Black Gay Men's Bowling League*. Oh no. No, no, no. Not here. Not now. God must really be straight after all.

"I've never seen you here before," I said like he broke into the building. "Why are you here?" He looked as though he found me amusing.

"The reason I'm in a bowling alley is because I came to bowl." I could tell from the look in his eyes that I was coming across as crazy. He put his wet hands under the dryer right in front of him. "So, you bowl too?" I couldn't say anything. "Okaaay. See ya." He snatched a paper towel out of the dispenser and quickly dried his hands. He tossed the paper in the garbage with a hook shot and walked to the exit while I washed my trembling hands way past *Old McDonald.* The germs must be totally destroyed by now. "Wait a minute," he said. He faced me with his hands on his hips. "Now I remember. You were the one at the rally. The one who was scared to come in."

"I wasn't scared." I gave him my best defiant stare but I couldn't meet his eyes without looking away. I turned my back on him and stuck my hands under the automated dryer and waited the two years it takes for one of those things to blow you dry. I listened to the electric breeze of the dryer, the patter of water in the sink, and the hiss of the regulated air freshener. The sound that never came was him opening the door and leaving.

I glimpsed in the mirror, and there he was, still watching me with his hands on his hips. He had a condescending smile like he was dealing with a wayward boy. He took a step closer and I thought my heart would stop. Again, I was plagued with the terrible fear that my porn would be discovered when I died. I really must find a better spot to hide my porn. Maybe I could keep it in a safe deposit box.

"I'm Emmanuel Keys." He smiled and nodded.

"Yeah, I know."

"And you are?"

"Here with somebody." He laughed.

"What's so funny?"

"I've never met a good-looking man with such bad manners before."

"In LA? That's a goddamn lie." He laughed again and it got on my nerves. I kept rubbing my hands under the lazy dryer. I could have just wiped my hands on my shirt but I didn't want to look like a slob.

"Why you got to be so cold, baby?"

"Don't call me that, man. It ain't even that kind of party."

"I'm sorry. I guess that was out of line." He wouldn't leave and I felt a responsibility to say something.

"I would shake your hand but my hands are wet." The dryer stopped. "I gotta go." I moved to the exit and he stepped in front of me.

"Are you still wet?" I either could not or would not walk away. "Let's try this again. I'm Emmanuel Keys." I shook his big warm hand and told him my name. My real name.

I never gave a new guy my real name before and cursed myself for making the exception. "Look, we're both here with people but..." He reached in his pocket and gave me a card. "... will you call me? It bothered me that you got away from me at the rally. And I hate it that you don't want to talk to me now. But don't let me go a third time. 'Cause if you keep on playing hard to get—I might just let you win."

"I'm not hard to get." I can't believe I just said that. "I mean— I'll call you later."

"Good, man. That's real good." He walked away and left me there with his expensive card in my hand. It suddenly became very precious to me and I put it deep in my pocket. I checked out his behind when he walked away and liked what I saw. Was he a top or a bottom? Wait a minute. I'm getting way ahead of myself. First, we have to get to know each other. I never felt the need to do that before.

Me and Tyrone got to know each other over the course of sexual escapades. There are plenty of things he still doesn't know about me, however. When I first met Tyrone I didn't give him my real name because there was no reason to. We did it in Griffith Park where we were both cruising the area. We did it again in his SUV when we saw each other a few weeks later at The Study. I don't usually go to The Study because all I ever see in that bar are sissies and old men. But that night, I didn't feel like driving too far, so I took a chance and was glad I did. I can clearly remember the SUV because he wanted to make sure his kids didn't find any condoms there in morning. But I really didn't work on getting to know Tyrone. It just happened as a byproduct of meaningless sex. Really hot, mind-bending, meaningless sex.

The same could be said for Kim. I met her at a straight club back in the days I used to go. We exchanged numbers and hooked up later. Like most women, the consummation meant more to her than it did to me and I could tell from the start that she was looking for a husband.

One night, when I had too much gin, and allowed myself to feel guilty because of her unceasing, demanding need, I told her the truth about myself to get her to go away. It didn't work. In spite of my disclosure we never got to know each other either. The only thing Kim knew about me was that she wanted me no matter how bad I treated her. And all I knew about Kim is she was a shield against a world that's hostile to gays. And every now and then, for just long enough to get what we wanted, we participated in the socially acceptable practice of exchanging recognizable masks.

As for Emmanuel, I didn't want to run away to Boston and marry him or anything. I didn't want to buy a loft with him and adopt two Chinese crack babies. I just wouldn't mind getting to know him a little better. That's all. I just wanted to do something right for a change.

I waited for our orders at the counter instead of heading straight back because I wanted to make sure where Emmanuel was first. I reasoned, because of the number of people in here, that I could easily sell the story of why it took me so long to get our food. Then I realized, with a laugh, there was no need to lie because I hadn't done anything wrong this time. I really did just go to the bathroom to wash my hands. I had been so used to coming up with cover stories that my mind was on automatic deception.

Emmanuel was with his bowling league, right in the middle lane, and they were thankfully a good distance away from us. There were about twenty of them in all. Emmanuel was entering names into the scoreboard so he didn't see me pass by. I scanned the other members of Black Balls and tried to figure out which one he was dating. He wasn't in a serious relationship, was he? He didn't seem like the type who would run a game but that's the type that always does.

Anyway, they were quite a group and all the men were attractive. Most of them were un-clockable but there were a few flamers in the bunch for certain and one major drag queen.

The drag queen let out a scream when she made a strike as if she had just won furniture on *The Price Is Right*. If the bowling shirts didn't give them away then she definitely would. Then again, they weren't really hiding, were they? People paid them no mind. A bunch of gay boys together is hardly an uncommon sight in this city. I marveled how they could wear those shirts in public. I was envious of their freedom.

I suddenly wished I hadn't come here with Kim and resented the company of my straight friends. Friends. Yeah, right. Emerson defined a friend as somebody you could be yourself around without the fear of judgment. My college days taught me there's a limit to being myself. Why do I have to fit into their world all the time? Why can't they fit into mine?

I approached them while Kim was pouting in her seat. "Don't worry about it, baby," I said. "Your inspiration has returned!" I smiled at her but she didn't smile back.

"Took you long enough," said Lamar.

"Yeah," said Tank. "We thought you got kidnapped by them faggots over there." Everybody laughed except Kim. She just looked at me.

"What faggots over where?" I said.

"Over there," said Stacie. "Look at 'em. There they go." I acted surprised like that was the first time I'd seen them.

"Black Balls," said Jennifer. "Lord have mercy. They everywhere."

"Uh. That's a trip. So how'd you do, Kim?" I said.

"Fine." She took my order from the tray without looking at me. I could sense an attitude and didn't want the others picking up on it.

"And which one of you losers took my turn?" I said.

"Nigga, you need to be grateful," said Tank. "You ain't the only man in the world that can roll a double, you know."

"You didn't mess with my ball, did you?" I said. I ran over to check on my baby.

"Man, please. My fingers can't fit in them little biddy holes."

The scoreboard had been cleared and a new game had started. "Who won?" I said.

"We did," said Stacie.

"Look at that. I leave for two seconds and the world falls apart."

"It was more than two seconds," said Kim. That remark left a chill I couldn't disguise with a joke.

"Ok," I said. "Let's eat." We all dug into our food in silence. I couldn't help but look at Emmanuel when he got up to bowl. He babied the ball into the gutter. Oh well. Nobody's perfect. He covered his face with his hands and shook his head while his friends pointed at him and laughed.

"Look at that big faggot right there." I couldn't believe it. It was Kim speaking. "All that man laying up with another hard-legged nigga. I mean girl, please." I stared at my food.

"Honey, I'm glad they together. Let 'em keep their AIDS in the family 'stead of spreading it to us," said Stacie.

"For real, though," said Jennifer. "I read all about it in *Essence* magazine."

"Yeah, girl. It was in *Sister 2 Sister,* too. Now, look here. If they get them diseases, doing things they ain't got no business doing in the first place, then that's their problem. But if they spread that shit to women who don't know no better then that's just wrong."

"I know that's right," said Jennifer. I shoved several french fries in my mouth.

"And what the media doing jumping all over Isaiah Washington for?" Lamar said. "That brother ain't got to go around accepting faggots just because Hollywood tell him to. Man should not lie with man. It's an abomination. Say that in the Bible." Oh look. The weekly adulterer quotes the Bible.

"The Black Gay Men's Bowling League," said Kim. "Alrighty then." She stood up and cupped her hands to her mouth. "Well, go head, girlfriend!" Several patrons, including Emmanuel, turned to look at us. He looked confused as if trying to figure out if Kim was talking to him or not. He saw me sitting next to her and turned to say something to his friends. I pulled Kim back down to her seat while she and the others laughed.

"Kim, knock it off."

She yanked her arm away from me and got in my face. "Why?" I didn't know what to say.

"You better listen to him, girl," said Jennifer. "Some of them sissies be knowing how to fight. They'll get wild on you in a minute."

"I wish one of them shit-packers would even think about coming down here," said Tank. He looked back at them and the drag queen made a point of showing us she was staring at our table. Emmanuel had sat down and wasn't looking anymore.

"Don't look back over there, Tank," I said.

"Why?" Kim said. "You don't think Tank's man enough to kick a faggot's ass or what?" My throat closed up and I was in dire need of a drink. Everybody waited on my response. I felt like I showed up early to a party and the people I knew hadn't got there yet. "Well? Answer the question."

"Kim, I don't think it would be prudent to instigate a confrontation. If they don't bother us then why bother them? What's the matter with you?"

"I could ask you the same question," she said without missing a beat. "I didn't know you were so fag friendly. What are they calling it these days? Oh, yeah. Gay adjacent. Did you know that, Lamar? What about you, Tank?"

"I'm not adjacent to anything. What's the matter with you?"

"You asked me that already." She glared at me, daring me, egging me on. The rest of them stared at me with no expression. Just looking at me like—

"Is there a problem?" Oh no. Oh God, no. It was the drag queen speaking directly to Kim. This queen stood easily six feet five. She sported Joan Collins shoulder pads stuffed under her bowling shirt. Her pointy, cone-shaped breasts aimed forward like ready weapons. Her broad face, and square jaw line, was caked with foundation too light for her skin, giving her the ashy appearance of an angry corpse. She had mean slits for eyes that were framed by her barely there, yet highly arched, *Memoir of a Geisha* eyebrows. She wore a neatly trimmed afro that glistened with sheen and her thick lips were painted stop sign red. She flamboyantly flung her forest green scarf across her bulging Adam's apple and continued in a hoarsely feminine voice. "What's the matter, honey? Cat got your tongue? Bad kitty." An embarrassed Emmanuel stood next to her. He avoided my eyes and I feared that he'd think I was a part of this mess. He gently took the drag queen by the elbow to lead her away but she shook him off. "Well, come on now, sweetie. You seemed like you had something to communicate to my party. I thought I would make it easier for you so you wouldn't have to yell across the room anymore. Like a fool. So go ahead, dear. Say it to my face." Again Emmanuel tried to lead her away and again she shook him off. "Uh-uh, Emmanuel, I'm gonna give this bitch a chance."

"Bitch?" Kim said.

"Did I stutter?" The drag queen took off her rhinestone Teletubby ear rings and gave them to Emmanuel who reluctantly took them.

"I might be a bitch but at least I'm a real woman," said Kim.

"First of all, there ain't no might. You really is a bitch. Bitch. But one day, if you grow the fuck up, you might be a real woman. Okaaay?" She reached across me and snapped her fingers in an elaborate configuration in Kim's face. "Ok."

"All right, now! Go 'head, Zelda." There was the African pride man with the dreads and glasses from the rally. Unlike Emmanuel, he was looking dead at me. Their whole group had come over and surrounded our table.

"You gonna let that faggot talk to your woman like that?" Lamar said.

"Mr. Man," Zelda said to Lamar, "Which one of these skanks is *your* woman? The ugly one or that fat one? Let me know so I can talk to *her* like *that*." Lamar sat there looking at Zelda with his mouth hanging open.

"Oh hell naw," said Stacie. "Sissy, I ain't fat. I'm pregnant."

"Who's the father?" Zelda said.

"He is!" Stacie said. She pointed at Lamar.

Zelda bowed her head. "My condolences." Lamar still didn't say nothing. He probably didn't know what condolences meant.

"Why you gotta be picking on the females?" Tank said. "You a man up under all that makeup. Least ways you supposed to be. So be man enough to deal with another man." Tank stood up and towered over Zelda. He put his finger in her face. "And you don't want none of this, hear?"

Emmanuel stepped in front of Zelda. "Can I have some?"

Dear God. Please don't let Tank kill my new husband. We have Chinese crack babies to raise. In Jesus' Name I pray. Amen.

Tank looked back at Lamar and chuckled while pointing his thumb at Emmanuel. Now a crowd was gathering. I saw the lady who rented our shoes at the counter getting on the phone and looking our way. "Can you have some?" Tank said. "I don't feel comfortable with a dude like you asking me some shit like that."

"Don't worry about it," Emmanuel said. "I only sleep with men."

"Blam!" All the Black Ball members said, while they slapped each other's hands. They all buzzed in the background while Emmanuel stared Tank down. They constantly made smart aleck comments like, "Dr. 90210? We have a face for you fix. Yes sir. It's been cracked." Zelda lowered her voice like she was an announcer on one of those nature shows and said, "Straight men can sometime be punked out in their natural habitat. Observe."

Tank chuckled along with the homos laughing at him like it didn't bother him. He looked at his wife and back at Emmanuel. The kids who ran by me earlier had their elbows propped up on the table beside us with their faces cupped in their hands. Their parents were behind them and half the bowling alley crammed in our direction to see what would happen next. At the entrance, I saw the cops arrive. Thank God. Now this circus can end.

"You need to watch who you talking to, faggot," Tank said.

"Why don't you beat my faggot ass?" Emmanuel said.

"I don't want to touch you. You might bite me and give me AIDS."

"You will die of being a dumb-ass nigger before I ever die of AIDS." The two cops were moving people out of the way so they could get through.

"Let's go, Manny," Zelda said. *Manny?* "The cops is here." Emmanuel glanced nonchalantly at the approaching cops and looked Tank up and down.

"I guess it's your lucky day, huh?" Emmanuel said. Why did he have to say that? Tank threw a left, that Emmanuel blocked, and he punched Tank hard in the gut. Jennifer screamed as Tank doubled over and made a grunt like he was about to throw up.

"Nobody move!" said the cop. Lamar lunged at Emmanuel but Zelda punched him in his nose and he fell flat on his back. The kids laughed and their parents grabbed their little hands and pulled them away. The Black Ball members scuffled with police who were shoving their way to the action. "Get out of the way or we'll take your asses in!"

"Don't push me, motherfucker!" One of the members said. "Prime Time, everybody!" At that moment, several Black Ball members whipped out their cell phone cameras and pointed them at the police. The crowd was out of control and somebody knocked Stacie down. She landed on her stomach.

One cop pulled out a nightstick and the other pulled a gun. Tank went at Emmanuel again. He ducked and tagged Tank in the jaw with an uppercut. Tank's head snapped back and he dropped to all fours. Emmanuel eyed him with the calm of an experienced hunter.

"Leave him alone!" Jennifer screamed. Tank grabbed Emmanuel by the belt in a sad attempt to get off the floor. He looked up at him while blood poured from his mouth.

"I'm gonna kill you, faggot!"

"I'm the faggot who's beating your ass." Emmanuel grabbed Tank by both sides of his head and kneed him in the face. His unconscious head hit the floor.

Kim grabbed me by my shirt and shook me. "Do something!"

"I wouldn't do a thing if I were you," The African pride man said. He stared at me, all bad, like he had my number. And I suppose he did.

That's why I hit him.

I knocked that dread-headed faggot into the middle of next Kwanzaa. His dashiki flung up over his head when he landed on the cops and they all went down. It was a powerhouse strike. Emmanuel looked at me and I was ashamed. Lamar was out cold. Stacie crouched on the floor next to him, trying to revive him, and holding her belly. Kim and Jennifer were on their knees trying to calm Stacie down.

But now I had a real problem. Now Zelda was mad at me. That big bitch jumped on me with a Patti LaBelle yell and grabbed me by the throat. I couldn't breathe. My lack of air was so sudden that it was like somebody turned off a faucet. I didn't know which was worse: having my mother find my porn or the cops telling her I was killed by a drag queen. I tried to say something but no sound would come. The cops got off the floor and more policemen ran in. Their guns were drawn.

The place was deafening with hollers, laughter, and screams. I twisted this way and that way in a panic to get Zelda off me but it wasn't any use. She backed me to the table and pressed close against me so I couldn't kick. I tucked my chin to get space between her hands and my neck but it wasn't working. I might have heard Kim scream my name. Zelda leaned closer and smiled. "Yall fucked with the wrong faggots today." I smelled cigarettes on her breath. Her eyes filled with tears. Her face shook and she squeezed my throat tighter. "I get so tired of you motherfuckers fucking with me." I couldn't inhale. Tears rolled down her cheeks. She looked at the ceiling and hollered to God. "I get so tired of these motherfuckers fucking with me!"

My world is blurred. Pandemonium fades. I think Emmanuel tells her to let me go. I don't know. Pain subsides. It's not so bad after all. I think Emmanuel tries to pull her off me. I don't know. I could be dreaming that. I could be dreaming this whole thing and when I wake up I'll be happy. My life will be easy and I'll have friends. And children. I'll tell Rayford and Annie and Johnny what a crazy nightmare I had. Melodious. Everything is melodious. Then I remember Jesse Chuma. And then I wanted to live.

I decide in a split second to use leverage against Zelda. I grabbed her hairy forearms and let her push me down to the table. I squirmed on my back and side until I can work myself up to my knees. Now I was high above her head. I could hear my temples throb. I got to one foot and, with the strength I had left, I pushed off the table and jumped on her. We fell into a pile near Kim's direction. Zelda released me and I gasped for air. I was still disoriented but while I was coughing I heard somebody scream,

"My baby!"

10

This Means War

The baby was dead. I didn't go to the funeral but Kim did. She was supposed to call and tell me about it later. The phone's ringing. It's probably her. I'm not going to answer. Time passed and I looked out the window. Today's a gym day but I've decided not to go. I'm afraid people might recognize me from the news. They didn't say my name but my face was on the screen and anyone who knows me would recognize me.

Emmanuel was arrested for involuntary manslaughter. I stare at his card and wonder if he's out on bail yet. I pick up and dial the first few numbers but I don't have the courage so I hang up the phone.

I call in to work instead and tell McGhee I'm taking another day off. If he knows about the bowling alley, he doesn't let on. I think he knows because he's being nicer than usual. He's never nice. He knows. I probably won't win the car. A few minutes later the telephone rings and I let the answering machine pick up. I assume it's Kim but it's Tammy instead. She says some kind of nonsense about how she misses me and she's praying for me. Prayer never worked for me.

I prayed when Stacie complained of cramps and her pants got wet with fluid. I guess God was busy watching *The 700 Club* or mixing hurricanes for homos because the baby died anyway.

When I pushed Zelda off me we tumbled into Emmanuel and we all landed on Stacie. Zelda was in custody with a very stiff bail. I told them I didn't want to press any charges but Lamar did. Since it was his dead baby that was more than enough. Tank spent a few days in the hospital and to hear him tell it he was overcome by fags like a mighty lion taken down by hyenas. He never admits how it was just a one-on-one fight and he lost to a better man.

I'll never go bowling with those people again. I just couldn't go back to pretending things were normal. It's a shame because I loved spending time with them. It was a part of my life that remained untouched by this gay stuff. Now it's all over me like a disease. Poor Stacie.

There were enough witnesses to testify that the gays approached us first. Yes, Tank threw the first punch but a woman lost a baby because of a group of militant homosexuals. That's how the conservative radio talk shows were spinning it. Gays against motherhood and all that stuff. Emmanuel didn't have a chance in the court of public opinion. The big gay groups, the white ones with money, came to his support with lawyers and such. He was charged with inciting a riot, public endangerment, and like I said, manslaughter. Laurence has been a big help. He's always in the know and he's been keeping me abreast of things.

It was Laurence who told me that Emmanuel's gay rights office had been bombed. It was Laurence who told me that Emmanuel Keys was dead.

I listen to a lot of classical music on the radio these days. I listen to it because it's soothing. I recognize some of the songs from commercials and such. I know a song or two from Beethoven but that's about it. And that's fine. I just need it in the background.

There was a ton of hate mail against Emmanuel's group. It was right up the public's alley. It personified everything straight people feared about gays. That we wanted to be women. That we were a danger to the family. Laurence said the group got threatened everyday but, since this happened, it had picked up considerably.

I wished I had done more and didn't know how to feel. I didn't know Emmanuel well but his death is an incredible loss to me. His death is the end of potential and makes me wonder if I'll be happy at all. Sometimes things happen in life and you say... this is it. This is the one. Yes, I'll be able to go back to work. Yes, I'll be able to laugh. I'll even find new passions and maybe feel good for a few days in a row. But I will never be happy again because this time life has worn me down.

I should have visited him in jail. I should have written him or called him earlier. I should have told him I had nothing to do with this. I would have never laughed at him. He was the only man who even made me even consider coming out. I didn't do any of the things I should have done because I was waiting on the perfect time, off in the future, when things would be easier to handle. The big illusion of life is that the perfect moment never comes. It doesn't exist. The perfect moment is a myth.

Lamar probably did it. Gay groups have called for his investigation but that's just a bunch of faggots complaining about something. Gays will never get the same respect that civil rights groups get. This isn't a lynching by the Klan. A straight couple's baby is dead and that homo got what he deserved. That's the way they see it.

It's like that whole thing with the *Jenny Jones Show* years and years ago. Some gay guy made a pass at a man on national television and got himself shot. Straight people actually understood how that could happen. They never talked about how the murderer had been flirting with his victim before they ever got on the show. He was trying to kill the faggot in himself, is all. So no matter how many gay groups bitch and moan and call for justice, nothing's going to happen to Lamar. Lamar's the straight man, the real man, who lost a baby because of some sodomites. I doubt the cops are even looking at the evidence that hard. They'll find the killer of Biggie Smalls before they worry about what happened to some faggot. In Boston, this Nazi fucker walked into a gay bar called Puzzles Lounge and started chopping up folks with a hatchet. When they tried to stop him, he pulled out his gun. Why are faggots always target practice for the assholes of the world?

Lamar used to love to talk about the shady types he met on his trucking routes. *Watch it, nigga. I know Tony Soprano.* Some of these truckers haul more than just legal goods and when you're in that world you learn a thing or two about another side of life. I think Lamar got some of his trucking acquaintances to hook him up with the proper people and that's how they killed my man. My man, I said. That's funny.

Tyrone called. I don't feel like dealing with that moron right now. I should at least call Stacie but what would I say? Tell her I know how she feels? I don't. Tell her it'll all be all right? It won't. There is absolutely nothing to say to a woman who has lost a child. Anything that comes out of my mouth would be euphemisms at that gates of Hell.

The phone rings and I check the Caller ID. It's Kim. She hangs up when the answering machine comes on. Something should really be done about Kim. Kim should pay for what she's done. If she had just kept her mouth shut then none of this would have happened. She knew what she was doing and she did it anyway.

I hate being bothered with fag hags. Unless I'm watching Karen Walker I never find fag hags amusing. Apparently, I'm the only gay man on the planet who just doesn't get Kathy Griffin. Kim's not really a fag hag, per se, but just like a fag hag, she hung around a gay man because she thought something was missing in her life that only a sissy could provide. Fag hags remind me of those white kids in high school who only wanted to hang around you because you were black. You could be the biggest nerd in the world but at least you're black. And to those lonely, insecure kids, being black represented some type of freedom from their stifling existence. They hung around blacks because they wanted our "cool" to rub off on them and feel somehow less afraid of the world. I always resented those white kids, with their forced ebonics that I didn't even speak, because I knew they weren't really looking at me. They were looking at what I represented.

That's what the fag hag does. I hate those drunk straight bitches who waddle over to me in the middle of a gay club and say something like, "Gay gays love me." Do they? "I have so many gay friends." Is that right? "I love to come to the gay clubs because the music's so good." They don't play good music at straight clubs? At all? "I love coming to the gay clubs because you know there's not going to be any pressure. And there aren't going to be these jerks hitting on me all night and I don't have to be worried." And that's the problem with the fag hag.

They don't want to be worried. So they use they use the faggot as a buffer against a world where they have to be an adult in. They want to siphon off our special "magic" or *joie de vivre* or whatever these bitches think we have that they can't find with a straight man or within themselves. They like our "wit" and we're so "easy to talk to" because we don't want to fuck them like a "real man" does. So they see us as these surrogate sisters who they can curl up with and hide from the world. Forming a real friendship, with a real woman, would be too challenging because they're threatened by other women. So they use the faggot as a play girlfriend. Starting a relationship with a straight man, who expects far more than a hug, is too risky for them. They might get hurt or have to do some actual work in the relationship.

So they run about, collecting sissies like Ken dolls, so they can have the benefit of male companionship without the demands of being responsible for their happiness. Why should I let a straight woman use me like that? If they don't like the music in their own clubs then let them buy a CD. If they don't want men making passes at them then quit whining about being alone. If they can't find anybody who's easy to talk to then maybe they don't have anything to say. There are so few places gay men can go in this country without persecution. Our clubs belong to us alone, which is why they call them gay clubs in the first place. Let straight folks find their own amusements and don't let a fag hag waste your time.

You've got your own problems. What kind of friendship do you really have, when the main thing you've got going for it, is the absence of sexual tension? Some of you homos even let the fag hag help you choose a lover. If she likes him he stays; if she doesn't he goes. You idiot. How could you let a man-less heterosexual give you advice on how to choose a gay man? Think. Use your head for something else besides a meat warmer. I can hear you now. "But so and so's my true blue buddy. That's my girl right there. We've seen each other through thick and thin." What are you, a fucking therapist? "Oh but so-and-so loves me." You're wrong. I'm telling you that right now. The fag hag doesn't love you. She loves what you represent.

Like Kim. As I've said, she's not a true fag hag but she's fag hag adjacent. There is something broken in that bitch which is why she latched on to me in the first place. And out of some warped sense of responsibility, and an inability to love myself, I tolerated that needy heifer far too long. And now my man is dead.

I think something should be done about that. And Tank. And Lamar, too. If they had just minded their own damn business and left them faggots alone then that baby would still be alive today and so would Emmanuel Keys. And who suffers for it the most? We do.

These conservatives on the local talk shows are a trip. They want to blame the gay community for the death of this baby like they blamed John Kerry's loss to Bush on us. Senator Kerry had that election handed to him on a silver platter. We were fighting a controversial war and there were absolutely no weapons of mass destruction. He had everybody from Michael Moore to P. Diddy urging people to vote for him. If he couldn't win with all that… then he just couldn't win. I think it's Senator Kerry's fault he lost the election and not mine. Maybe if the Democrats would grow some balls then they could win something else besides an opinion poll. It's like the baby. Yeah, that's right. It's like… it's like that time that lady killed her kids by pushing the car in the lake. And she told the news media, in a weepy voice, that a black man kidnapped her children. And people ate it up because they're always willing to believe the worst about a nigger. And they're always willing to believe the worst about a fag. And I'm both.

Emmanuel was right. There really is a war going on and we need to win it. I should have been a braver soldier. And now he's gone. But now I have a chance to make it right. Now I have a chance to fight. I am ready to enlist in this cultural war. And my first targets are Tank. Lamar. And Kim. Then those morons on my job.

~~Tank~~.

~~Lamar~~.

~~And Kim.~~

~~Then those morons on my job.~~

11

Tank

I went to Tank's place about a week after the baby's funeral. I expected questions about why I didn't attend the service and Tank didn't disappoint me. "You should have been there, man. People asked about you."

"I sent them flowers and a card."

"That's all?"

"That's enough. You'd be surprised how much people don't want to be bothered with folks at a time like that. I called Lamar and asked him if he needed anything and he said no. What else do you expect?"

"Kim was there."

"That's Kim's prerogative. I don't do funerals, Tank. I just don't." Hell, I didn't even go to Emmanuel's funeral. Did he really expect me to show up for some baby I had never even seen before? There was an uncomfortable silence then he picked up the remote and clicked his wide screen set on. He channeled surfed for a while: *CNN. BET. ABC. HeadOn.*

"I hate that commercial," Tank said.

"But their product is amazing." We both laughed. He reached down to the coffee table to get his beer but he was still stiff and the effort caused him pain. "You need help?" He hesitated. He needed help but didn't want to ask for it. "Let me get it." I picked up the beer and noticed it was warm. "You want another one?"

"Yeah, all right, player. Thanks."

"I'll be right back." I exited the wood-paneled den and walked down the stark white hallway lined with family photos. He and Jennifer had two boys around the same age, eight or nine, something like that, I've never been one of those people who can look at a child and tell how old it is. Anyway, the boys were holding a little league trophy, smiling wide in their dusty uniforms, and there was another one with the boys and Tank on a fishing trip holding up three tiny fish. It was so damn corny.

Jennifer and the kids were out shopping and I knew I couldn't do it here because I'd get caught. She knew I was coming over and, with my finger prints all over the place, and my saliva on the beer can, I'd be making the job far too easy for CSI. This had to be out of the house and this had to look like an accident. Would anyone put it together if three people who knew me died within days of each other? Maybe, maybe not. One of the benefits of being in the closet is that people don't really know much about you. Not even people who see you everyday.

Maybe murder is a tad too much. Perhaps humiliation would be enough. The way they humiliated Jesse. The way Rayford humiliated me. Still, Emmanuel Keys is dead. There has to be some kind of balance for that.

I got Tank a cold beer out of the fridge and, as I walked back to him, I couldn't help but wonder how I went from a guy who just wanted to get laid to a man who was ready to kill. I gave Tank his beer and watched him drink it. He swigged it and let out a sigh. "You know what, man?"

"What?"

"I've been thinking 'bout what you said and I understand. My daddy always hated funerals and didn't go to them either. He didn't want to face death. And that's your problem. You don't want to face death either." He was going to try to shrink me like he did with those At Risk youths who had to put up with his tedium on the threat of going back to jail.

"Yeah, maybe you're right," I finally said. "But so what? I mean, who the hell wants to face death?"

"Everybody got to face death. Even Jesus faced death."

"Yeah, well. If I could walk on the water and come back from the dead then I'd be able to face death, too."

He laughed. "Man, you a trip. Don't be blaspheming in here, though." Blaspheme? Where did that come from? It never ceased to amaze me how they could click their Christianity on and off like a switch.

"So how are you feeling, Tank? When you going back to work?"

"I'll do. My neck's still a little sore." He looked like hell. His lip was swollen and he wore a neck brace. He had several bruised ribs so his chest was wrapped. "If them faggots hadn't of jumped me, and fought like a man, then things would have been different." Jumped you? I guess if you tell yourself a lie long enough you'll eventually begin to believe it. The power of affirmations. "I got some leave time built up so I'll just use it early, I guess. My supervisor told me to take as long as I need."

"Uh-huh." We sat there watching college football for a minute in silence. "So what about you? How would you face death?"

"Like a man."

"What does that mean?"

"Like a man. Just like I say. Head on. Ready to go. Knowing I had done my best in life."

"I wonder if that's how that Emmanuel Keys faced it?"

"What you mean?" He looked at me funny.

"Oh, what am I talking about? Of course he didn't face death like a man. He didn't even know it was coming." I laughed and stretched out my hand so he could slap it. "Lamar, got that fag-got good, didn't he?" Tank laughed nervously and tapped my hand as hard as his injuries would allow.

"Yeah, he got him. Eye for an eye. But keep that on the down low, hear?"

"Oh, I will." I had never really been sure before but know I knew. Lamar killed Emmanuel.

"I wish I had the hook up like that, though. There's a lot of fuckers at my job who need to take a long vacation. Know what I mean?"

"Yeah, I hear you, man. That ain't nothing to play with, though. That's something for emergencies."

"How do you make arrangements for something like that?"

"I don't know. You have to talk to Lamar 'bout stuff like that. Check this out." He turned up the volume and focused on the set, which was his way of saying the subject was closed.

This was going to be more involved than I thought.

"You know what we need to do?" I said during a commercial.

"What?"

"We need to get Lamar and take him out somewhere. It'll be good for him."

"I can't get around much myself."

"It'll be good for both of you then. I know you're tired of looking at these four walls."

"Yeah. But Jennifer wouldn't go for it. Not 'til I healed up."

"So what? Whose the man around here? You or your wife?"

"Nigga, you sound like a fool."

"Then it's settled. I'll call Lamar. Where's the phone?" I was making this up as I went along but I knew the next part of the plan was talking to Lamar.

12

Lamar

They had a nice place in Crenshaw, right near the mall, off Victoria Lane. As long as I had known them, I'd never been to their house before. It was just one of those things. They would always say, "You should come over to the house sometime. We could put on some steaks."

And I'd always say, "That sounds good. Just let me know." But they never did and I never pressed them on it because I wasn't all that interested. It was just one of those things people said. This time I went to their house because I had a reason to. I had always been smart. I knew that if I just put myself in the situation, and exposed my brain to the problem, then I would come up with an effectual course of action.

Lamar opened the gate on his front door and let me in. The place was still filled with plants and flowers. I wonder if he knew what condolences meant now? Everything from big green ferns to tiny white lilies and roses with baby's breath lined the sides of the living room, and crowded the coffee table, and filled the corners of the kitchen. I even saw my arrangement. There were cards, so many cards in neat rows, on table tops, the mantle, or just piled in a chair. Lamar scooped a stack of cards out of the way so I could sit down. He gave me a beer and turned the tv up louder.

"Stacie back there?" I said.

"Yeah, but she don't feel like no company right now. You know how it is."

"That's fine, man." I didn't come to see her anyway. "How you holding up?"

"Shit, man, it change from day to day. You know how it is." Why does he keep saying that? "It's fucked-up for real though. But at least we already got healthy children and we can always have more. It was a boy."

"Oh, man. I'm sorry." Why did I say that? Would I be less sorry if it were a girl?

He nodded his head and looked at the screen. "Yeah. We already got three girls and I was all set for a boy. That's all right though."

"Listen up. Me and Tank were talking about getting you out of the house. Getting you some air. You game?"

"Game? You sound like a white boy." I laughed. I hated it when he said that. A real Oreo wouldn't be this close to you, you fucking moron.

"Well, what do you think?"

"Tank feeling better? He sounded tore up when I talked to him."

"He's not one hundred percent yet but he's looking to stretch his legs. It'll be good for him."

"Yeah." He kept flicking the channels. He wasn't convinced yet. "That sissy fucked his ass up good, didn't he?" He laughed and I joined him. He laughed so hard tears came from his eyes. "Whooo. I needed that. Yeah, I need to mess with ole Tank about that when he feel a little better."

"I wouldn't if I were you. He might talk about that drag queen knocking you out cold." I laughed and reached out my hand for him to slap it but he left me hanging.

"Now, wait just a goddamn minute. Ain't no fucking drag queen knocked me out. You hear me? I got a bad back. I don't sit in a office like you. I work for a living."

"Ease up, Lamar."

"I work hard loading a truck and driving for hours at a time. All right?"

"I thought the trucks were loaded before you took off."

"They is, motherfucker, but sometimes I got to help out here and there. 'Bout three years ago, I was loading some gears, and I turned the wrong way, and that shit tore my back out. All right, mister? I done had three back surgeries in the last three years. I got spurs in my back. When the doctor opened me up he said it looked like a porcupine in there. All right? I'm in constant pain all the goddamn time."

"You never mentioned it before."

"Hey. Look here. I don't go around whining about my job the way you do. Ain't my style. I'm just saying."

"Doesn't look like it affects your game. You roll a bowling ball just fine."

"Hey! Look here! The doctor. All right? You know the doctor, Mr. Big Brain? The doctor?"

"What about him?"

"All right. The doctor. Hear what I'm saying? Told me. All right? Bowling was good for my back."

"Oh ok then."

"Ok then motherfucker. So when that faggot hit me in the nose and shit? That pain shot right down to my spine. You can't do shit without a spine. You hear me, nigga?"

"Yeah, man."

"So when that faggot hit my nose that wasn't nothing but a thang right there 'cause Mr. Lamar can take a punch."

"Uh-huh."

"But these bones are interconnected and shit. Like that." He locked the fingers of both hands together and shoved them in my face. "You ask a chiropractor about something like that." Yeah, that's what I'm gonna do. Call a chiropractor and ask him if your nose is connected to your spine. "And anybody can throw a sucker punch. I can knock Mike Tyson out right now with a sucker punch." So what? Anybody can knock Mike Tyson out right now with a sucker punch. "When I got hit in the nose, what had happened, in effect was—I was temporarily paralyzed. And my brain shut my body down so I could recover. And that's the real deal right there. Ain't no faggot did shit to me!"

"I hear you, man. I'm not here to upset you."

"Well shut the fuck up then."

Stacie walked in the room wearing a faded pink bathrobe. "Lamar, stop it, fool."

I rose to embrace her. "Hey, Stacie. I'm so sorry about everything." She hugged me back and leaned into me.

"Thank you. We got your flowers."

"You probably shouldn't be on your feet. Come on." She sat down with me on the sofa while Lamar kept his eyes on the tv. "Look, guys. I just wanted to say... I'm sorry about my part in all this." And I was. "If I did anything to—"

"He was stillborn."

"Oh."

"Yeah. The women in my family are late but not that late. And I ain't never been that late before neither. Maybe I knew the truth but didn't want to face it. You see what I'm saying?"

"Yeah."

"All that mess at the bowling alley just hurried up something that had already happened. But the baby was dead already, honey. It wasn't your fault or anybody else's. That's what I been trying to tell Lamar but he won't even talk to the doctor."

"Shut up, Stacie."

"But the baby was stillborn. Don't you know what that mean? He was dead anyway. You shouldn't have—"

Lamar got up and stood over her. "I said shut up!"

"Lamar, calm down, man," I said. Stacie ran from the room and we could hear her door slam down the hall.

Lamar sat down back down in his raggedy recliner and pressed the remote. He stared at the channels zipping by with tears in his eyes. "I don't care what she say. I don't care what no doctor say. If it wasn't for them faggots, my son would be here today." Tears fell on his remote control. "I think you better go, man."

"Sure, Lamar. I'll call you in a couple of days."

13

Kim

None of this would have happened if I were out of the closet.

" *... I've been out and I've been in and being out is better.*" Anything is better than the way I'm living now. *"Because I was in the closet, I made poor choices in men."* Like Tyrone and Dante: a married man and a psycho. And that nobody actor with his paranoid delusions. *Being in the closet caused me to maintain friendships with viciously homophobic straight people that I should have let go of a long time ago."* I should have found friends with who I didn't have to hide around. People who would have loved me no matter what.

If I had just accepted Emmanuel's invitation at the rally that day then maybe we would have been together instead of attaching myself to a needy woman in order to feel normal. There's no escaping it. If I was out of the closet then Emmanuel would be alive today. My need to hide put him in a situation that wouldn't have existed if I had just been myself. There's only one thing to do.

I have to come out of the closet.

I call Kim and she picks up on one ring as she always does. "Hey, you!" I can't believe she has the gall to sound perky.

"We need to talk," I say.

"Ok. You want to have lunch at the mall again?"

"No. My place." I could tell by the silence she was shocked. I had never invited her to my place before.

"Ok."

It took her about forty-five minutes to get to my condo. She called me from outside because she was having trouble finding parking on the curb in front of the building. I went downstairs to let her in the garage and park in the empty space that I rented next to my car. It was more expensive but parking is nonexistent in this town and it's money well spent if you're used to having company. She got out of the car and threw her arms around me.

"Don't start. Come on." She followed me to the elevator where we saw the old man with the Old English sheepdog.

"Hi, there," he said.

I don't speak but Kim does. "That's a beautiful dog."

"Oh thank you. He's my best friend."

"That's sweet," said Kim. "How old is he?"

"Fourteen years. That's pretty old for a dog, you know." I jabbed the elevator buttons as if doing that would make it go faster.

"What's his name?" Kim said.

"Omega."

"Ooh. What a unique name. Hey, Omega. Hey, boy." She tried to pet him but he growled. She huddled next to me and grabbed my arm.

"Don't worry," said the old man. "He's not gonna bite you. Are you, boy? Go ahead. Pet him again."

"That's a bad idea, Kim." Good Lord this elevator's taking forever.

"No, really. Give him a stroke."

"Ok," said Kim. She reached down to pet Omega and this time he snapped at her. She screamed.

"That's the story of your fucking life," I said.

"Gosh, I'm sorry. He doesn't usually do that. I'm awful sorry. Bad dog, Omega. Bad dog." The old man smiled at Kim hugging my arm. "You two look like an old married couple."

"We're not," I said. "I'm a faggot and she's in love with me. I called her here to dump her once and for all." The elevator doors opened and we stepped outside. Kim had that stupid, hurt look on her face.

As the elevator doors closed, the old man said, "I'm in 12-D!" She trailed behind me like that would delay the inevitable but I didn't wait for her. I entered my living room and left the door opened for her and got myself a Sprite. I sat down on the sofa and waited for her to come on in. She finally appeared, like a gimpy Avon Lady, and leaned on the door way.

"Why are you being so mean to me?" She started to cry.

"Dry your eyes."

"Why are you doing this to me?"

"Hey you! Stop that goddamn crying!" She looked at me in fear and like magic her tears went away. "Don't worry. I've never hit a woman and I'm not starting with you. Get in here and close the door." She quickly obeyed and sat down in the kitchen. "What were you up to that night, Kim? Huh?"

"I saw you."

"You saw me what?"

"At the bowling alley. When you went to get the food. I had to go to the bathroom."

"And?"

"And I saw him come out of the men's room. And I read his shirt. And then I saw you come out next. You were in your own world, you didn't even notice me. You walked right by. You ... you were glowing." She took a big breath to steady herself. "I've heard stories about what gay men do in restrooms and truck stops and places like that."

"Look. I didn't do anything in there except wash my hands and that's the truth."

She didn't look like she believed me. "And he gave me his card but it was nothing sexual. And you're not my wife. Hell, you're not even my girlfriend."

"But you don't mind letting people think I am, do you?" I didn't know what to say. "Is that all I am to you? A beard? A disguise?"

"Don't give me that mess. You get off on it, too. You like the attention you get when we're together. It makes your weak ass feel like you're more than you really are."

"Look who's talking."

"He gave me his telephone number. All right? I bet you get numbers all the time. I don't know what in the world you do when we're not together."

"Yes, I get numbers but I throw them away because I don't want anybody else." I didn't respond. "So I followed you. I knew it was wrong but I followed you. I saw you go to the food counter to get our orders. And then… I saw you lean back and look at that man like you were watching the sun rise. I've never seen your face that way before." She looked off into space and lived it again. "I've seen you angry. I've seen you passionate. I've seen you sarcastic and mean. But I've never seen you… happy. And I knew you would never look at me that way. No matter how hard I tried. No matter how hard I prayed. There was nothing I could do. I would never be enough for you. And you know what? It was worse than if I caught you in bed with another man. I caught you *in love* with another man." She tried to stop crying and failed. "Then I walked right past you to back to our table and you didn't even see me. Again. I was so tired of you not seeing me. And I'm not stupid. I know there's something going on with that Tyrone man, too. Where was he that night? You told me he was thinking about joining the league. You told me you met him in the bowling alley. How come he and Mabel weren't there bowling with us then?" I was too tired to come up with a lie. "So when I saw that man standing up there with all those fa… those gay men, I felt like… why should *they* win? *I'm* the woman. I'm not bad to look at. I'm not *trying* to be a woman, I *am* a woman."

"He wasn't trying to be a woman either. Is that what you think of me? That I wish I had a vagina?"

"Do you?"

"Kim, this conversation is a waste of our time. You will never understand me and I will never appreciate you. I'm sorry for all the trouble I've caused but let's be clear."

"I love you."

"Then that's your problem 'cause I don't love you back. And I never even pretended I did. And not loving you doesn't make me a bad person. It just means I don't love you."

"How can you brush me off so easily? Like I was nothing?"

"Brace yourself, honey, but I have the right to reject you. That's the problem with you modern gals. You've got no problem having an open mind until shit stops going your way. Quit feeling sorry for yourself. Women are always talking about their bodies and their rights. Yall love to say stuff like, 'This is my body. Keep your hands off me,' or 'This is my body, I'll kill this baby if I want to,' well... this is *my* body. I'll share it with another man if I want to."

She stared at me. "You won't share it with Emmanuel Keys." Then the bitch had the nerve to smile. I wanted to kill her. I really did. The only thing that stopped me was the old man in the elevator. He was a witness. I wish I could say it was something more than that but it wasn't. I only let her live because of a technicality. Besides, where would I hide the body?

I got up and took her by the arm. "It's time for you to go."

"Get your hands off me, faggot! I hope you die of AIDS."

"I'll be so glad when a new disease comes along so straight folks can find a new insult. Let's go." I opened the door and pushed her out.

"Stop it, faggot, I'm going!" Her voice echoed down the hall way. "Hey everybody! Want to see what a down low sissy looks like? Open up your doors right now!"

"That's not going to help, Kim."

"It's going to help me. Open up, everybody! Look at this so-called man turning down some damn good pussy here!"

"Let's not exaggerate, dear." I heard doors opening down the way. A teenager poked his head out and his mother came into the hall to see what was going on.

"Hide your son, miss! He's a good-looking boy and you live on the same floor with a real live faggot!" The mother pushed the boy back in the door. I could hear it lock as we passed by. Several other neighbors came out. I never got to know these people. Anyone who lives in a large complex knows you never really get to know your neighbors anymore. You can live right next door to someone for years and never even know their name.

Nevertheless, I recognized faces from the elevator, the mailbox, and the laundry room, and they, in turn, recognized mine. And now, even though they didn't know my name, they would definitely know who I am.

I'm the faggot who lived down the hall.

Kim was in rare form. If she had ever shown this much backbone before, then who knows? Maybe it could have lasted a little longer or she would have left a little sooner. "Take a good look, ladies! Real live shit-packer here! You can't tell by looking these days! So pay attention!" People were laughing. Some had their hands over their mouths. Some had their portable phones presumably calling the police or the management. "Sorry about this," I said in a quiet voice as we continued our long walk to the elevator. "Everything's all right, folks. We're leaving the building." Some nodded their heads in sympathy. Others looked at me like I smelled. Oh well. I wanted to come out of the closet and I guess this is a good place to start. Home is where the homo is.

When we reached the elevator, I pushed the button, and for the first time since I've lived here, the doors opened right away. That was the good news. The bad news is that it was full of people. I ushered Kim through the doors. "Get your hands off me. I don't know where you been. Keep your fag juice to yourself!" One lady got off the elevator. The others stared at the floor numbers or straight ahead. Quite naturally, Kim picked this moment to break down and cry. "Why don't you love me? Why? Just tell me what to do."

"Go away." The digital readout of the elevator counted down our descent.

She laughed in a way that sounded bitter and tired. "You want me buy a dildo? Huh? Strap it on? You want to take turns being the bitch?"

"Not with you," I said.

Somebody behind us laughed and Kim went crazy. "You think that's funny? You a fucking faggot, too? Like him? Why the fuck did I move to LA? Fuck you! Laugh at that, bitch! Fuck all yall!"

The elevator opened on the parking level and I pushed her out. "Stop it. You're making a fool of yourself." I turned to the people who were coming out of the elevator behind us and said, "I'm sorry about this. I really am."

She slapped me. Her ring scratched my face. "Don't you apologize for me! You should be apologizing to God. Fuck you!"

A white girl with a bicycle gave me a tissue. "You're bleeding" she said. And so I was.

"Thank you." I dabbed my cheek with the tissue and looked at the red spot.

"Are you all right?" The white girl said.

"I'm fine. Come on, Kim."

"You need me to call the police?" The girl said.

"Fuck you, you white cunt!" Kim said. "There ain't no point in trying to steal another black man 'cause this one hates pussy! Even white pussy! Get it?"

"Kim, stop it!" I grabbed her to calm her down. She snatched away from me and hit me across the head in a frenzy. I turned her away from me to pin her arms and she stomped my feet.

I heard the white girl on the phone. "Yes, I need the police at..."

"Fuck you, you ugly white bitch!"

"You hear that? The police are coming. You want to lose your job?" She calmed down a bit before collapsing into a mess of tears. "Just get in your car and go. I'll let you out of the garage. It's over."

She stopped struggling and I let her go. I walked her to her car while everybody stared. Someone else had already used their remote to open the parking gates and a line formed at the exit. The girl behind us was still talking on the phone and I couldn't really hear what she was saying.

We made it to Kim's car and she opened the door. Then she spat in my face.

"Oh my God," I heard somebody say.

Kim smiled. "I hope you meet that dead faggot in Hell one day." She got in her car. She revved her engine loud and the noise echoed through the deck. I looked ahead at the other vehicles inching out of the exit with the passengers carefully checking both ways of that precarious blind spot.

I wiped her spit off my face with my clean, white handkerchief. I knocked on her window and she rolled it down. "This is a tricky exit," I said. "I'll guide you out."

"Yeah, make yourself useful. 'Cause you damn sure wasn't no use in the bedroom. With your little-ass dick."

"Ok." I jogged to the exit where there were two cars waiting. I looked both ways like a good little sissy and trotted across the street. I waved to the first car that it was clear to go. The grateful driver waved at me and headed straight down Western. I signaled to the second car that all was well. The driver honked his horn in appreciation and drove along his way. Everybody hated that exit. I've complained to management about it myself, you know.

Then came Kim's car.

I held out my hand that she should wait. She shot me the bird and I watched out for traffic. A line of cars built up behind her. She honked her horn impatiently, trying to peek around the blind spot herself, and pulled forward. I frantically gave her the "stop" sign.

She shrugged her shoulders because, from her point of view, the street was clear. But everybody in this building knows that's such a tricky exit. As I said, I've spoken to management about it on a number of occasions. My name is even on a petition to get a signal light there so people won't get hurt.

Then, I saw a big-ass truck.

You know the kind that hauls Volvos on it. I waved to Kim that all was well. And little miss thing was so upset that she screeched right out of that parking deck.

14

One Down. Two To Go.

Thank God for witnesses. Each and every last one of them. All I had to do was stand there and be horrified while the police talked to all the cooperative eyewitnesses. Such as the drivers behind Kim who saw her speed into oncoming traffic. The reliable little white girl who had called the cops on her in the first place. The passengers in the elevator who saw how upset and unreasonable she was. The neighbors on my floor who confirmed she was cursing loudly in the hallway. Many of them had already called the manager who identified me to the cops as a good tenant who never caused any trouble. And then there was that adorable old man. He told the police he knew there was something wrong with that girl because his dog snapped at her and his dog never snapped at people. I was able to tell the cops that they could find him in 12-D. He also told the police what I said about dumping her because I was gay. I easily agreed when the police asked me about it because now I was out of the closet. If I had known that the truth could be this convenient I would have told it a long time ago.

I didn't worry about Stacie and the gang asking about Kim. They only knew her through me and didn't see her that much anyway. Yeah, the news crews came but what's one more fatal accident in the City of Angels? Lamar and Stacie had their own problems to worry about and Tank mostly watched the sports channels. It was as if she never existed.

Now was the time to call the guys and arrange something potentially dangerous. A fishing trip? No. That's so overdone and I don't know a damn thing about fish. Let's see. I don't hunt and they can't very well die in the bowling alley. Finally, I came up with something that might be workable. I called Lamar first.

"Hey, Lamar. How's it going?"

"Hey, man. I'm all right."

"How's Stacie?"

"She 'bout the same. You know how it is."

"Yeah. Well give her my love. Listen, call Tank and put us on three-way."

"Hold up." I waited.

"Hello?" Tank said.

"What up, nigga?"

"Hey, Lamar. How you holding up, man?"

"I'll do."

"How Stacie?"

"She 'bout the same."

"You're on three-way, Tank, so don't say something stupid," I said.

"What up, fool? What yall getting into today?"

I suggested that since we had all been through a great deal and we were all off for a few days that maybe we should go to the gym for a solid workout. The bowling alley held too many memories and a workout would be good for Lamar's health. It was even better for the back than bowling was. I also told Tank I could bench press more weight than he could, which stirred up his constant need to prove how much of a man he was. "Come on now, player. They don't call me Tank for nothing. You don't want none of this."

"Well let's put a little money on it. Unless you want to punk out because your boo-boos still hurt."

"When and where?" Tank said.

"Let's go to Bally's," I said. "I can get you both a guest pass for the day. Maybe even a week. You've got to take this bullshit tour while they try to sell you a membership but it doesn't last that long. And then we could work out. There's a steam room in there too, Lamar. It'll be good for your back."

"You said Bally's?" Lamar said.

"Uh-huh."

"Ain't that a faggot gym?"

"Not this one. This is the one by Roscoe's Chicken and Waffles. There ain't nothing in there but big-breasted hootchies pumping up for rap videos. And what the fuck would I be doing in a faggot gym anyway?"

"All right, motherfucker, calm down. I was just asking."

"Well, you're asking the wrong damn question. I get mine. I don't appreciate that shit."

"Excuse the fuck out of me, nigga."

"All right, players," said Tank. "We all friends here. Chill out now." We chilled and they agreed to meet me at the entrance of Bally's at 2:30. I figured they wouldn't get there until about 2:45 or 3 o'clock. That gave me enough time to prepare if I got there ahead of schedule but first I had some shopping to do.

I arrived early at the free-weight area and worked up a good sweat in my new windsuit. It's a beautiful black jacket and black pants with a red stripe. I was having a good time working out and it was so refreshing to look at men directly instead of using the mirrors. There were more than a few guys I never approached before because I was scared of looking gay. That was no longer a concern. I collected a few phone numbers and kept working out until the ones I was waiting for came in.

There they were. Dante and Henry right on time. Henry saw me first. He whispered to Dante, who noticed me then avoided my stare. That's fine. I can wait. I saw an old friend while I was waiting. It was Anderson, the security guard from the bank.

"What's up, man?" I said. He looked like he didn't know me at first but then his face lit up with recognition. He gave me that halfway hug and shoulder bump thing that the straight thugs do and we talked for a bit. He looked great in his tank top and form-fitting sweats. I spotted Dante in the mirror trying to act like he wasn't looking at us.

"I thought you worked out at Gold's," I said.

"I do. But they was giving out these passes at the bank so I thought I might check it out."

"I get it. You've been through all the boys at Gold's so you're hungry for fresh meat, right?"

"You crazy." He glanced below my waist. "I hadn't seen you around lately. Been missing you."

"Oh yeah?"

"Yeah."

"Well, I tell you what, Anderson." I gave him my card. "My bed is probably a lot more comfortable than that secret mattress of yours. And Lord only knows what's on that thing—"

"You a trip."

"—so give me a call and maybe we can hook up tonight."

"For real?"

"For real."

"All right then."

"Look, I see some friends of mine I need to talk to so I'll see you later. All right?"

"That's cool. I got to hit the bike anyway." He took another look at my card. "How do you pronounce your name?" I told him. "Oh, ok then. I'll holler at you."

"Bye." Anderson was no Emmanuel Keys but life goes on, now doesn't it? I set my eyes on my targets and approached them directly, speaking to Henry first. "What's up, fellas?" Dante stared at me from under the squat rack. Henry was spotting him. Dante seemed surprised that I even spoke to them. Maybe he's remembering when I ignored him at the rally. "Hadn't seen you guys in a while. The last time I saw you was when they were having that rally."

"Yeah I remember." Dante said. "But you was busy."

"I heard they blowed that dude up," said Henry. "That true?"

"Yes."

"Man. That's fucked up, homes. You knew him?"

"I didn't know him that well but I considered him a friend. So how much can you squat?"

"Three eighty."

"Really?"

"Yeah, homes."

"He could do more than that if he wanted to but he lazy," Henry said. He ruffled Dante's hair.

"You the one," Dante said. He swatted him with the towel and Henry laughed. They saw me watching them, in this little slip they had allowed themselves, and made an adjustment. Dante went back to being macho and crossed his arms.

"We be done in a minute."

"Can I work in?"

"Well…" Henry said. "We kinda doing a superset. But there's another squat rack over—"

"Look, man. I'm sorry about the last time. I didn't mean to disrespect you, Henry." His eyes popped wide.

"How you know my name?"

"I see you guys working out all the time. I heard you talking to each other. Don't worry, man. I'm not a stalker."

Dante chuckled a little. "Oh, I ain't the type of nigga that worry 'bout shit." He patted his gym bag. "See what I'm saying?"

"And what's your name?" Henry said.

"I'm Tyrone. Look, there's no need for drama. I didn't know yall were a couple."

"And how you know it now?" Dante said.

"I just figured. You know. Body language."

"Body language? What the fuck you trying to say? Look here, I don't even come off like that. My shit is correct. All right? You got the wrong one, homes."

"I meant no disrespect. And Henry? Forgive me if I crossed a line the last time. Some guys are into threesomes and stuff. You know what I mean? And you just never know what the deal is but, uh..." They just looked at me. "I think you guys are great. Hell, I want what you have one day." I extended my hand and, after a while, Henry shook it.

"You want to let him work in with us?" Henry said.

"It up to you," Dante said. Henry looked around the gym.

"Maybe we can do more than just work out," I said.

"Turn around," said Henry. I complied. I could see Dante staring at my cheeks in the mirror. He nudged Dante's arm. "Can I have some, too?"

"Whatever make you happy, baby."

"You not gonna get mad at me, papi?"

"I already got a taste. Your turn. And it's soft, too."

"Yall can tag-team this ass if you want to," I said. "We can go back to a hotel or whatever."

"I want to watch, papi," Henry said. "I want to watch you fuck him and then make him come on my belly." Yikes.

Dante glanced about to make sure we had reasonable privacy. "Let me watch you first, baby. I want you to grind this black bitch up under all these weights. Like you watch me last time? You remember, baby? We went home and made good love that day, right?" Henry giggled like Fester Adams. "You know your papi love you and give you the world, right?" Dante looked at me and said gruffly, "How much weight you want on here?"

"Let's wait a minute."

"Wait for what?" Henry whined.

"Yeah, wait for what? You came to us, remember?"

"Yeah, I know but…" I looked at my watch. "I need to get this supplement out of my car that I take before I work out."

"But I want it now." Henry said. He kicked a barbell on the floor so hard that the weights rattled. If he hurt is foot then he didn't let it show. Dante snapped him with his towel.

"It's ok. I'm here." Henry looked at his foot and appeared to be counting to calm himself down.

"Hurry up," he said. "I want it on my belly."

"Shh," Dante said. "Shush now. Keep your voice down. It's ok. Be a good boy for papi, hmm? Hurry up, homes."

"Uh… I'll be right back." I went to the entrance and saw Lamar and Tank through the glass door waiting outside. I pulled fifty bucks from my sock and gave it to the guy at the counter. "Here's a guest pass for my friends here but we don't have time for the tour. They're not gonna join anyway. Just let us through, ok?"

The guy took the money. "Hurry up before my manager comes out."

"Thanks." I bounded through the front door and surprised them. "What's up, fellas? Yall been waiting long? Hurry up. I arranged it so we can skip the tour." Lamar was about to say something but I turned my back on him and walked on in. They followed behind and I nodded at the guy at the counter.

"Welcome to Bally's, gentleman." They gazed around, like they were in the Land of Oz, and I sped ahead.

"Wait up, man. Damn." Lamar said.

"Check it out." I nodded my head at two women up on the second level. They were wearing leotards and working out on the pec deck machine.

"Aww sooky sooky now," said Tank.

"Damn. Fuck bowling," Lamar said.

"See? I told you. Stick with me fellas. Oh Tank? There's this guy back here, that's smaller than you, and says he can squat three eighty."

"Bullshit."

"No it's true. You think you can take him? Maybe we can make some money."

"Where he at?"

"Come on. Keep up, Lamar." We came upon Dante and Henry who were surprised to see me with people. "Look here, fellas. These are some good friends of mine who just came in." I gave Henry a look. "And they're down." I quickly made the round of introductions. "But here's the thing. Tank doesn't think anybody can squat more weight than him. He's willing to bet money on it, too. Let's see who's bluffing then we can take care of that other business."

"No, you said we could go now. That's not fair." Henry said. He stuck out his lip.

"Yo, Henry," said Dante. "Keep it together." Tank and Lamar looked at each other.

"There's some money in it," I said.

"Yeah," said Tank. "Some money for me. No offense, amigo, but I can tell by looking at you that you can't push more weight than me."

Dante chuckled a little. "Amigo?"

"Well, let's cut the chatter and put your money where your muscle is, Tank. You'll like squats, Lamar. They're good for your back."

"I wanna talk to them bitches upstairs, though."

"They'll be down here. They always come down to the free weight area. Every time. So anyway, I'll go first. Tank, help Dante put two more forty-fives on there. Henry, gimme a spot."

I stretched while Dante and Tank loaded the bar and Lamar took a seat on a neighboring bench.

"Watch me carefully," I said to Henry, "I might need help with the weight."

I unzipped my track jacket and showed off my tight, white Domino's t-shirt. I got it from that vintage store I saw before I met Kim in the mall that day. Henry couldn't take his eyes off the Domino's symbol. Then I unsnapped my track pants, whisked them off, and unveiled the true glory of my He-bitch pants.

"What the fuck?" Lamar said.

"What's the matter?"

"What the fuck you got on, man?"

"What? These? These are workout shorts. The kind body-builders wear. What's wrong?"

"You look like a bitch. That's what's wrong."

"Lamar, you're not used to working out in a gym. That's all."

"You don't look like you used to getting no pussy in them shorts," Tank said. "You gonna wear that for real?" I looked at Lamar in the mirror. He was studying Henry who wouldn't stop looking at my ass.

"Look. Tank. If you want to get out of our little competition just say so. Don't blame it on the shorts."

"There's nothing wrong with the shorts!" Henry yelled. "They're pretty!" A few people looked in our direction.

"Shh," said Dante. "It's ok."

"Pretty?" Lamar said. "Did this motherfucker just say pretty?" Tank laughed loud and Dante looked at him.

"What's so funny?" Dante said.

"Say what?" Tank said.

"Ok, come on, Henry, gimme a spot." I took my place under the bar. "Ten reps, Tank. Here I go. Spot me, Henry, watch me now." I squatted down with two hundred and seventy pounds on my back. Henry grabbed my waist and stepped in close.

"One," said Henry. I looked in the mirror and saw him staring at the Domino's sign on my back. "Two." The mirror revealed Lamar watching Henry closely. "Three." Dante stared at Tank and, not being one to back down, Tank stared back. "Four." I halted at the bottom.

"You need help?"

"Yeah," I said. "Here we go." I squatted up again with Henry almost riding me.

"Five," Henry said. His breathing became labored. "Six." I could feel him get hard behind me. In the mirror, I saw the two fine girls from above come downstairs.

"I'm done," I said, "Help me up." Henry grabbed me by the waist to help me up and I returned the weight to the rack. When he stepped away from me, they could see the front of his shorts poking out.

"What the fuck?" Lamar said. Henry covered himself with both hands. Now the girls from upstairs were looking, too. "This nigga dick got hard!" Dante saw the girls looking at us. Henry still stood there with his hands over his privates. He was hyperventilating and began to cry.

Tank laughed.

"Man, what kind of shit we done walked up into?"

"Yo, you better leave him alone, homes! I tell you one time!" Henry cried uncontrollably. "It's ok, baby. Papi here."

"Baby?" Lamar said.

Tank kept laughing. The fine girls behind us laughed, too.

Henry exploded. "Stop laughing at me!"

Lamar grabbed my arm. "I thought you said this wasn't no faggot gym."

"To tell the truth, Lamar, I'm the wrong faggot to ask," I said. The girls behind us said something and giggled. Lamar looked at them and punched me in the face. I went down by Henry's feet.

"All this time?" Lamar said. He walked slowly towards me and Henry. "What was you doing? Laughing at us? My son got killed 'cause of you faggots."

"Hey, I ain't no fucking faggot, homes," said Dante.

"That your fat Mexican boyfriend right there?"

"I'm Salvadoran!" Henry screamed.

"I don't give a fuck what you is, bitch! I killed one of you faggots before and I'll do it again!"

"I told you, homes!" Dante went for his gym bag. *Dante always packing, child. That fool sleep with a gun. Brush his teeth with a gun.* I got off the floor and pulled Henry near the exit. "I told you!"

One of the fine girls screamed. "He got a gun!"

"Hold up, player, easy now," Tank said.

Dante jammed the gun under Lamar's jaw. "You a big man, huh? You think you kill my baby?"

"Wait a minute," Lamar said.

"You think you kill my Henry?" Dante pulled the trigger and Lamar's brain splattered on the mirror. He didn't even make a sound. Screams filled the gym and people ran for cover. I squeezed between Henry and the wall because that was the safest place to be. Dante pointed the gun at Tank and I closed my eyes. I heard Henry holler for Dante. Then the shots and the screams. People ran for the exits.

15

Born Again

"Child, have I got news for you," Laurence said.

"Could it wait 'til tomorrow? I gotta to go back to work in the morning and I need a good night's rest."

"No, Blanche, it can't wait! Do I ever call you without rhyme or reason?"

"Uh..."

"Shut up. Guess what?"

"What?"

"Dante and Henry are on the run, honey. It's just like Bonnie and Clyde. Without the woman."

"What are you talking about?" I put some ice on my lip while he talked nonstop. I was still swollen from Lamar's punch but he won't be punching anybody else, or calling hit men, ever again. I enjoyed knowing the scoop before Laurence did, for a change, but of course I couldn't tell him I already knew the story. Sometimes it's best to just let Laurence talk.

"I told you that boy was crazy. Now ain't you glad you listened to me?"

"Yes, actually."

"Why you say it like that?"

"Like what? You gonna tell me or not?" Laurence did have a few new tidbits to share after all. The mother of Dante's baby reported her car stolen and it was found abandoned in Las Vegas.

"You know what they say," Laurence said. "What happens in Vegas stays in Vegas."

"Gee, Laurence, I never heard that before."

"Shut up." A massive manhunt was launched but they haven't been found so far. Laurence said that Dante had become a member of MS-17, a notorious Latino gang, when he was in prison and they're probably the ones hiding him. "Oh yeah, child. Can you imagine? All them fine-ass tattooed Papis? Bunched up in the desert to keep each other warm at night as they hide from justice. Mmm-hmm. Color me Menudo. Is that a sawed-off shot gun in your pocket or are you happy to see me?"

I felt sorry for Dante's baby growing up without his daddy. I felt sorry for upsetting Henry also. I hope I didn't push him too far over the edge. I felt sorry for Jennifer and especially Stacie for losing a husband and a baby so close to each other. All the things I feel sorry about, however, are what they call in the military an acceptable rate of loss. What can I say?

Cultural war ain't pretty, baby.

Then Laurence babbled on about his contact in the media. "Your contact in the media? How the hell do you have a contact in the media?"

"Oh, child. This reporter I used to know. I only sleep with reversible men and he never wanted to be the bottom. Long story short: we'll always have Paris. Anyhoo, he told me that it'll be broadcast in most major outlets tomorrow that the cops see this as retaliation for the death of Emmanuel Keys. Dante's baby mama told the cops he was on the down low. Now that bitch has been squirreled away to protective custody because MS-17 frowns upon loose lips, honey. By cutting them off! But I digress. Didn't you know the deceased?"

"No, I didn't."

"But I thought that was one of your bowling buddies. Or some other pedestrian activity you engaged in to maintain the illusion of butchness. Or is it butcherosity? Which rolls better off the tongue?"

"Laurence, could you turn your flame down, please? The phone's getting hot."

"So did you know him?"

"Yeah, I knew him. He wasn't my best friend in the whole wide world or anything. Me and Kim bowled with him and his wife sometimes."

"And the other one?"

"What?"

"There were two guys right?"

"Well, yeah. Do you have any idea how big some bowling leagues can get? I can't keep up with everybody."

"So the guys you were bowling with wound up dead, who fought with Emmanuel Keys who wound up dead, and they were shot up by Dante, your South of the Border Happy Meal. My, my. Aren't we surrounded by tragedy?"

"I never knew or met Emmanuel Keys."

"Still, Blanche, that's such a coincidence."

"Weird, huh? So how's your daughter, Laurence?" He doesn't say anything. "Hello?"

"Uh—she's fine. Why do you ask?"

"I was just thinking the other day about how you always invite me to her birthday parties, and what not, and I never go. I feel a little guilty about that, Laurence. I don't want you to think I'm brushing you off. 'Cause this is a highly unpredictable world and a good friend like you is hard to find. So believe me. The next time you invite me to be a part of your daughter's life I will definitely accept. I have your address and I know where you live. So it won't be hard to find your family at all. How's your heterosexual bride these days?" There's a long pause. "Laurence? Are you paying attention?"

"Oh, um, child, I'm sorry, I'm watching *Desperate Housewives*."

"That doesn't come on tonight." There's another long pause.

"You ever heard of TiVo, Mr. Man?"

"Oh right. TiVo. You are so clever, buddy."

"So how's Kim? Haven't heard you talk about her lately."

"Oh, that whole relationship crashed and burned. I had to let her go. It wasn't fair to either one of us. And guess what, Laurence? Congratulations are in order."

"Congratulations on what?"

"I have finally decided to come out of the closet. I no longer want to live my life like there's something wrong with me. You ought to try it sometime."

"Is that right?"

"Yes, it is."

"Why? I don't need to tell folks my business. I shouldn't be expected to walk around yelling, 'I'm gay! I'm gay!' any more than any straight person goes around advertising their sexuality twenty-four hours a day."

"Well there's a couple of things wrong with that argument, Laurence, ole buddy. First of all, straight people already *do* go around advertising their sexuality twenty-four hours a day. From our billboards, to our videos, to our news coverage, to even your precious *Desperate Housewives*—we are bombarded with the message, from kindergarten to graduate school, in church life and our secular life, that men and women should chase each other, desire each other, fight for each other, and even kill for each other. It's a message that's constantly repeated whether you want to hear it or not. And this endless pursuit of man after woman, or vice versa, is the very thing that makes the world go 'round. They write songs about it. They organize campaigns around it. They make laws about it, ole buddy. In fact, I'm sure a court of law would have a bit of a problem awarding custody of your 'baby doll' to you—should you and your heterosexual bride ever go your separate ways. So never get divorced, ole buddy. Ever. And before the event of your wife's untimely death, God forbid, you'd better make damn sure it's in the will that you should get custody of your 'baby doll.' Because your in-laws, who were willing to ignore certain things before, might come up with other ideas if your heterosexual bride is no longer a factor. So you see, straight folks don't *have* to wear a sign that says, 'I'm straight, I'm straight,' because, Madge—you're soaking in it." I wait for him to respond but he doesn't. "So let's say you're Gay. Or Lesbian. Or Transgendered. Or Bisexual. Or just a Single Straight Woman who doesn't feel like buying into the program. Where does that leave you? That brings us to the second part of your faulty reasoning. Straight people don't have to justify or explain their sexuality because they run the whole goddamn world except select parts of New York and California. And even those lucky homos find life vastly different once they venture outside of their gayborhoods.

"Homophobia is the one thing that unites straight folks of different races and religions who wouldn't normally agree on too much at all. So we need people like me to yell, 'I'm gay, I'm gay,' because the universe is a big fucking place—and I deserve to be here, too."

I'm certain he's hung up this time. This pause is longer than all the others. Indeed, this pause has slid into a silence that gives me time to think about things. Like how I need to make a new life for myself. And this new life has no place in it for people who are ashamed of being like me. Finally, I say, "Good-bye, Laurence."

"Good-bye." He hangs up and I know I've become like one of those people who stop doing drugs so they can't hang around their cocaine friends anymore. I'll never hear from him again. And that's fine. I won't have any trouble out of him either.

The next morning, I head into work and get a warm reception from my favorite secretary. She's on the phone as usual so I give her a piece of paper and go through the second security door. She laughs when she reads it and I give her the thumbs up sign.

I head to the chalkboard and see that Tammy and I are in last place. Remarkably, everyone else is not that far ahead given the time they've had to work. Ted and McGhee are in first place with $10,000. Gary and Charles are in second place with $8,000. And Tammy and I ring in at $5,000. Four thousand dollars of that figure was made by me before I left work a week ago. This hallelujah heifer has only sold $1,000 in one week. Pathetic.

The cars are being presented today by the CEO of the company and the Jaguar dealer. If I want to get that car, I'll have to make at least $7,000 today. This is going to take some planning but I think I can pull it off if I can motivate the Christian.

Everybody's busy on the phones when I get into the sales room. Everybody but Tammy. The others wave at me and I wave back. Tammy doesn't see me because she's sitting there at her desk reading her fucking Bible. "What are you doing?"

"Ooh, Lord have mercy! Welcome back!" She jumps up and wraps those trunks around me and squeals like she's seeing a long-lost relative. I don't hug her back. She senses the tension and releases me. "What's the matter? You still depressed because them sodomites killed that baby? Lord have mercy. Well, I got a scripture for you. 'In the world ye shall have tribulation but be of good cheer; I have overcome the world: John Chapter 16, Verse 33.' "

"How come you're not on the phone, Tammy? Don't you ever get tired of being the worst salesman here?"

She flinched. "Oh. Ok. Now, I know you've been through a lot—"

"Uh-huh."

"—but don't let the devil use you as a mouthpiece. 'The tongue is a flame of fire. It is full of wickedness and poisons every part of the body. And the tongue is set on fire by Hell itself: James Chapter 3, Verse 6.' "

"That's sweet." I go to my cubicle, take off my blazer, and put it on the back of my chair. I get my coffee cup and say, "Walk to the break room with me, dear."

"All right. I could use a little snack myself. Even though Lord knows I don't need it." Then she laughs like she's seen the Second Coming of Richard Pryor. I put some papers on McGhee's desk when we pass by on the way to the break room. "What's that?"

"Just a memo."

"I didn't get one."

"I didn't give you one."

"Oooh, child. Them demons is messing with you today."

"Uh-huh."

I hold the door for her to go into the break room first. We have a crappy little break room with a grass-green carpet that's worn in the center. It has an old microwave that's always caked with crumbs. There's a relatively new coffee maker and a 16-inch color tv mounted high in a corner on the wall. I won't miss this place at all. I take my time fixing my coffee because it's all part of my morning ritual and this is the last ritual I'll be having here. Oh, I'm not going to kill them. That whole kill-all-your-coworkers thing is so last week. Besides, I wouldn't do anything to hurt poor Gary. Nature has done that already. I just want to have a little fun before I go. And I want to drive away from these suckers in that brand-new car.

Tammy studies the vending machine like she's Solomon trying to figure out which whore the baby belongs to. She decides on a Ho-Ho and says, "This'll keep me until dinner. I really don't eat that much. I don't know how I keep holding on to all this weight."

"Because you keep holding on to a bucket of chicken."

"Say what?"

"Sit down, Tammy." She sits and I decide that my coffee has reached the perfect balance of cream and sugar. I cut off the tv and join her on the black plastic couch. I sip of my coffee, she bites her Ho-Ho, and we look at each other for a spell. "So how's it been going?"

"Oooh, child, the devil has been busy in here today. And all last week. And the week before that, too. 'He prowls about like a ravenous lion seeking whom he may devour: First Peter, Chapter 5, Verse 8.' "

"You know, that's amazing."

"What's amazing?"

"How you can do that."

"Do what?"

"Perfectly spit out those scriptures, chapter and verse, like that. I mean the Bible is a big-ass book and you've got it memorized, Tammy. That's quite a feat. If this was *Who Wants To Be A Christian Millionaire,* you could have bought yourself a President by now." She laughs and I wait for her to stop. "Now if you can memorize all that then you can memorize your sales script. I want you to have the same confidence on the phone that you have with the Bible. How did you first manage to do that? Hmm? Where did you get this skill?"

"My daddy," she says. She tilts her head with a sad smile of remembrance. "My daddy knew everything about the Saints."

"Uh-huh. And is he still with us?"

"No." She grins so she won't look sad. "He's gone on to live with the Saints."

"You always talk about the Saints. What are you talking about?" And then she rattled off this list of Saint Jude, Saint

Hedwig, and Saint John the Baptist with a brief description to what each had contributed to the glory of God. "There's too many Saints to name right now, child. We'd be here all day. That's why you should come to church with me sometimes. They have more detailed study in Bible school. You could learn a lot."

"Is that right?"

"Oh, yes. And won't those ladies be jealous when I walk in there with a fine man like you on my arm." She touches my knee. "Don't you think it's time for you to find a good woman? I missed you when you wasn't here. You're so funny. Always teasing me. But I was mad at you that day you made me cry."

"Yeah. I'm sorry about that."

She got the strangest, most confused look on her face. I thought she was choking on a Ho-Ho. "Is something wrong?"

"No. I just never heard you say you were sorry before."

"Oh, I'm sorry about a lot of things. I'm sorry about losing this contest for one. Aren't you? I mean come on, Tammy. Think about the Saints! Don't you want to win a brand-new Jag?"

"Not really." I gagged on my coffee and she patted my back while I coughed. I had to lean away from her because the bitch was stronger than Samson. "I'm fine, Tammy. I'm fine! God damn it. I just had this shirt cleaned."

"You sure do use the Lord's name in vain a lot. I wish you wouldn't do that. I find it offensive."

"Well, aren't you little Miss Annie Assertive this morning? You know what I find offensive? I find it offensive, and just a tad bit stupid, mind you, that you wouldn't want to do what it takes to win a Jag. Why on earth not?"

"I can't fit into them little sports cars." I wished I had left the tv on so its noise could have filled the room. I didn't say anything for a time and Tammy nibbled her food while avoiding my eyes. I grabbed her hand. She covered her face with the other and cried.

"Why didn't you say so?"

"Would you admit something like that?" I suppose I wouldn't. She cried some more and I gave her my clean, white handkerchief.

"Pull it together, Tammy. Charles will be in here soon to steal packs of sugar." She gave me a weak giggle. "Look. I'm not trying to be cute so don't be offended by what I say next. Ok?"

"Ok."

"Tammy—life must be very difficult for you this way. Don't you think things would be a little easier if you just lost the weight?

She wiped her eyes and looked directly into mine. It was the first time I'd ever seen Tammy angry. "Why should I have to?" I tried to come up with an answer and her direct gaze made me uncomfortable.

"Well—things might be easier."

"Easier for who? For you? For the teenagers who make fun of me in the mall? Who would it be easier for? I like the way I am. My daddy used to tell me I was big 'cause I was filled with beauty."

I squirmed on the plastic sofa. "Well—you're the one who talks about not being able to find a man."

"So what? I was probably just saying something to pass the time 'til the elevator came. You ain't the easiest person in the world to talk to, you know." My mouth fell open. "Sure, sometimes, I wished I could lose a few pounds but I ain't stressing about it. I like myself. I am made in the image of God. And I don't even want a man who can't appreciate that."

I gulped my hot coffee to take up the time while she continued to stare. "But—but you can use this contest to go to the next level. Don't you even like this job? The money you could make?"

She furrowed her brow. "No." She folded her arms. "No, I don't. I hate this stupid job. I hate trying to talk folks into buying stuff they don't want. I always wanted to work with kids."

"Then, Tammy, what the hell are you doing here?"

She shoved the last of the Ho-Ho in her mouth and swallowed. "That's a damn good question. I quit."

"Wait a minute! Calm down! I could still win that car!"

"I need to talk to McGhee." She stood up and walked to the door leaving me stupefied on the couch. She stopped at the door and turned around. "And you know what?"

"What?"

"You a real asshole." And with that she left the room.

16

The Finish Line

Gary won the car. At the last minute, he and Charles made a run on the board. Maybe this means there really is a God and Gary will finally get laid. And that's cool. There was a big presentation ceremony and the *Times* came to take a picture of them. I wasn't there to see it. Gary told me about it later. I left shortly after Tammy did and started my own company like I wanted to.

That was about ten months ago.

Tammy and I weren't the only ones to leave the office that day. Some of us, like my favorite secretary, were fired. That memo I gave her was a series of jokes at McGhee's expense. She was instructed to call Charles and read him the jokes right before lunch. They were things like, "How many McGhees does it take to screw in a light bulb? None. Ever since the divorce, he can't afford light bulbs. Why does McGhee's hair stick out on the side of his head? Because it's tired of competing with the hair in his nose. How did McGhee become the new boss around here?

Because the old boss loved his blow jobs." Charles thought it was funny as hell when the secretary told him the jokes.

McGhee didn't share their sense of humor. He overheard their conversation on his manager's phone which can tap into every other phone in the office. *I usually call Charles for a little gossip but McGhee's always eavesdropping and makes me hang up.*

After Charles won his new Jaguar he drove away from his old job in it. Gary told me the secretary cried and carried on so that security was called to escort her from the building. Now she'll have more time to spend with her baby and dress him in masculine sweaters. I gave McGhee my letter of resignation along with the memo tipping him off to the conversation. The car would have been a nice cherry on the top but life had other plans. And Gary deserved it. He knows I'm gay, by the way, and was completely underwhelmed by my dramatic revelation.

I used my savings and got a bank loan to rent some office space in this cheap-looking industrial building in Culver City. I got the hook-up with a distributor, thanks to Gary, and I sell subscriptions for magazines to businesses that have expressed an interest in them. I have a small staff, of mostly college students, who need the extra money and can work in the evenings from five to eight-thirty. I save money on salaries by paying only commission so there's a high turnaround but I weed out the losers. The sales force I'm growing is comprised of real talents who are just as money-hungry as I am. I don't know how long it'll take to be the next Robert Johnson but I'm making a few hundred dollars more than I did before. And my new secretary, Zelda, keeps things running smoothly.

I'd always felt bad about what happened to Zelda. I got up the nerve to go to a meeting at Emmanuel's organization. It was an awful reception. The African pride guy pointed me out when I snuck in late and sat at the back of the room. They were having a meeting about letting people know that HIV is still a problem even though everybody is babbling about bird flu.

Zelda was taking the minutes of the meeting at the front of the room. She had to be restrained by several members of Black Balls when she realized it was me. After things calmed down, I told them my story. I left a lot of things out, especially the stuff about Emmanuel, but they got the gist that I was out of the closet and I wanted to help as best I could. I apologized for my for my part in the bowling alley disaster and told them I never wanted to be on the wrong side of a fight again.

They met once a week and it would be another month or so before they stopped rolling their eyes at me. One evening, I told Zelda I was impressed with her speed at taking the minutes. It was the first time she smiled at me. She told me how her family kicked her out of the house when they caught her in her mother's clothes so she had to become good at office work right away. Not many offices were willing to hire her unless she dressed as a man, which was something she didn't feel she should be forced to do. She supported herself with odd jobs but nothing that really excited her. One conversation led to another and now she's my secretary.

Zelda taught me that my views about transgendered people were just as prejudicial as any straight person's. It's called internalized homophobia and apparently I've still got a lot of it floating around in my system. You can't spend most of your life hating yourself and expect it to go away overnight.

I told my mother I was gay and she blamed herself. She still loves me however and thinks I should see a psychiatrist. We have a ways to go and I couldn't imagine myself bringing a man home for Thanksgiving or something like that. Speaking of men, I had to put Tyrone down. He thought I was just trying to tease him at first but I told him I no longer felt comfortable with what we were doing. The sex was fantastic. If I kept seeing him I wouldn't have had the strength to just be his friend. So I had to leave him alone all together. He kept calling for awhile.

At first, I ignored the calls and let the answering service pick up. He'd just leave lewd messages that would always turn me on without fail. Then, I started deleting the messages as soon as I heard his voice but that made me feel like I was hiding in my own home. So I started taking his calls and all I would talk about is coming out of the closet. He stopped calling so frequently and now I never hear from him at all. But he hasn't learned. He's just playing the same game with somebody new. And I'm just two minutes out of the closet myself so I don't have the moral authority to judge anybody who still chooses to be in it. It's a frightening world filled with dangerous people and no one wants to feel like everybody hates them. I understand all that. To each his own.

I've spent a lifetime convinced that there was something was deeply wrong with me that had to be hidden or changed. I've hurt a lot of people and I've acted out sexually for a very long time. I'm not going to turn into this perfect person just because I've come out. But I'm ready for something new now. I'm ready for something else. I'm not ready for a lover or anything like that but I don't have to travel my new path alone. When I went to my gay rights meeting the other night, they were all smiling at me. Then, Zelda gave me a present. I haven't received a present from anybody besides my mother since I was a child. I opened the box and was thrilled to see my very own Black Balls bowling shirt.

I am just as screwed up as everybody else on this mud ball floating through space. But as much as possible, I want to win. In my own way, in my own pace, I'm headed for the finish line now. This will be my last entry in this diary for a while. I'm ready to move on with my new life and ending this diary will be a symbol of that. Who knows? I might doodle in it again if life gets interesting. But right now, I'm just looking forward to the routine. In spite of my resolve to live a more truthful life, I really can't be silly enough to let anyone read the contents of this book.

And it has far too many important memories to destroy. Let's see. I'll definitely have to keep it someplace safe. Maybe I can hide it next to my porn.

The End